First published in Great Britain by HarperCollins
Children's Books 2010
HarperCollins *Children's Books* is a division of
HarperCollins*Publishers* Ltd,
77-85 Fulham Palace Road, Hammersmith, London W6 8JB

Visit us on the web at
www.harpercollins.co.uk

1

ISBN-13 978 0 00 731350 1

Printed and bound in England by
Clays Ltd, St Ives plc

Amber Aitken

The CUPID Company

Heart to Heart

HarperCollins *Children's Books*

heart of the matter

The sky above Coral curved like the inside of a giant beach ball, dipping and fading to blue before gently dissolving into the ocean's horizon. She squinted at the edge of the world, her red-brown hair curled like a head of bedsprings, bobbing around her. The horizon definitely looked like the edge of the world. It was the edge of her world, anyway.

She scanned the enormous sandpit before

her. The beach that morning was full of children with their buckets and spades, making shapes out of the soft, warm sand. A boy dripping wet from head to toe raced out of the sea before flopping, belly-first, on to a patch of dry sand. He rolled left and right until every bit of him was gritty and yellow before tiptoeing up to where a woman stood waiting to catch a Frisbee. Before she could do anything to stop him he had given her a full-body hug. She yelped. He laughed gleefully.

The sky above was suddenly filled with a whirring sound and an aeroplane droned across the sky with a long canvas tail that seemed to flick and ripple in the wind. Coral stared with a wrinkled nose until it was almost overhead. The canvas tail had a message: BEST OF LUCK SARA AND JEFF... LOTS OF LOVE.

The aeroplane continued on its way, as if to the sun, pulling the flying message across the sky. Coral shook her head. She was suddenly annoyed. Just *who* had wished Sara and Jeff the best of luck? Would Sara and Jeff know?

"Coral? Coral, can you hear me?"

Coral turned towards her best friend. "Mmm?"

"You actually have to move the broom to make a difference."

Coral stared at the broom she held like a dance partner in her arms. There was a dent in her forehead from where she'd been resting against it. Her friend was right, she hadn't done much sweeping. The thing was – she hated sweeping the beach hut. Unfortunately, her friend Nicks hated sweeping too. So every week they were taking it in turns. It was just that it always felt like it was her turn.

"What's the hurry, Nicks?" Coral grumbled. After all, they were on their summer holiday.

Suddenly, and without warning, there was a loud *thump-whack* sound coming from the glossy red beach hut next door.

Both girls' heads spun in the direction of the hut. They stared, silent and blinking.

"Did you hear that?" whispered Coral.

"Oh yes." Nicks's reply sounded like a hiss.

"We didn't imagine it then?"

Nicks shook her head slowly. This wasn't the first time they'd heard strange noises coming from the neighbouring glossy red beach hut either. And yet they had never ever (ever) seen a single soul enter or leave the place. It was always locked up tight with its shutters closed like two sleeping eyes.

Just then a shadow flitted across the window, and then it was gone.

"Did you see that?" gasped Coral, her lips hardly moving at all. She didn't want the watcher to know she was talking.

Nicks nodded and gulped. She had definitely seen that.

They both stood still and silent, staring – almost wishing for another sight or sound because that might just offer some perfectly obvious explanation as to what they'd just seen and heard.

All of a sudden a dog started yapping. Both girls jumped like they'd been electrocuted. But it was only Romeo, Coral's Jack Russell pup.

"Romeo!" they both groaned aloud. Romeo took his guard dog duties very seriously.

"We're probably just being silly," said Nicks. "I'm sure the noises aren't anything." Nicks had always been a sensible sort of girl. She'd never been the type to get tangled up in an overactive imagination, and she didn't want to start now.

"But I definitely heard and saw something," insisted Coral.

Nicks shrugged.

"We've heard strange noises coming from the red hut before," insisted Coral.

"It's the first time we've *seen* anything strange though," replied Nicks reasonably.

"So what should we do about it? Who should we tell?" said Coral.

"Tell about what?" sighed Nicks. "We've no proof that there's anything strange going on.

OK, we've heard a few noises... so what?"

That was true. Coral thought a bit more about this. Nicks had a point: apart from a *thump-whack* and a vague shadow, what else did they really have?

"So what should we do?" she asked instead.

"We should finish cleaning the beach hut and then concentrate on Cupid Company business," replied Nicks sensibly.

Coral nodded. Of course Nicks was right. Cupid Company business should always come first. After all, it was what the hut was all about now.

Coral had inherited the hut from her Great-Aunt Coral, but it wasn't long before it had become more than just a beach hut. It had become home to the little business they had set up – the business of love and matchmaking. And so far, they'd had two success strikes – Coral's cousin Archie and Gwyn, and Charlie (daughter of the next-door beach hut owners) and Jake.

Coral sighed dreamily. The path of true love

could be a lot of fun. Still, for now, she'd better get on with sweeping. It was her mum who had issued strict instructions to keep the hut clean and tidy at all times. Maturity and responsibility – that's what it took to keep the hut, she had said. And her mum usually meant things too. Coral reached for her dancing partner, the broom, and sighed. Acting cool, calm and collected did not come naturally to her. Still, she would try her best to concentrate on Cupid Company business while she was sweeping the sand from the deck of Coral Hut, which was how she came to realise that there was no Cupid Company business! Quickly she pointed this out to Nicks.

"*No business* is the Cupid Company business we need to concentrate on," came Nicks's reply.

"Of course it is," mumbled Coral, keeping one eye trained on the sandiest corner of the deck. She would keep her promise to her mum, but she wouldn't take her other eye off the glossy red beach hut either. Something

11

exciting could happen, and she wasn't going to miss it!

"We are a professional matchmaking company," Nicks said, while buffing the hut's small glass windows. "At the Cupid Company, when we say 'All for love and love for all' – we really mean it!"

Now Romeo grabbed the end of Coral's broom and started a game of tug-of-war. Coral grinned and pulled back hard. Nicks was too busy to notice. She'd already started on her next job of the day: a list written on the paper attached to her foil butterfly clipboard.

"One, we need to advertise. Two, we need to distribute Cupid Company questionnaires. Three, we need to think hard about all the single people we know in Sunday Harbour," she said as she wrote.

Romeo finally won the tug-of-war and claimed the broom as his own. He was just about to disappear down the hut steps when Coral grabbed the end back to reclaim it.

Further along, a game of beach cricket had

started up. The players were laughing loudly and running about and both girls stopped to watch them for a few moments.

"You know, the problem with living in a nice beachy town like Sunday Harbour," grumbled Coral, "is that the single people out there are just too busy having fun to think about how lonely they actually might be." She frowned thoughtfully and leaned against her broom. "They make matchmaking very difficult indeed." Romeo sat at her feet and stared solemnly ahead like he knew exactly what she meant. "I mean, isn't being in love what life is all about? Could there be anything better? Nobody can play beach cricket forever, can they?"

"Too right," Nicks agreed. "But look, would you just give me that broom?" she said impatiently. "If you sweep any more slowly you'll wear a hole in the floor."

Coral grinned, handing the broom over cheerfully. "Sure, Nicky-Nicks. I'll tidy up the inside of the hut, shall I?"

But it wasn't really a question. Before Nicks could answer, Coral had dashed through the door. She simply loved being inside Coral Hut. With its whitewashed walls and the pretty rug of scrambling pink primroses, it hadn't changed much since her Great-Aunt Coral's days.

Coral sighed as she looked around at the walls decorated with gold-framed pictures of chubby cherubs and the two shelves with books of romantic poetry. The whole room was like a shrine to love. What could be better than that? *CRREEAAK!*

The sudden noise from next door snapped Coral out of her reverie. The sound was like furniture scraping. It really was a mystery. Coral shivered, even though it was warm. Perhaps she'd had too much sun. Or maybe it was time to head for the safety of home.

home is where the heart is

It was still morning when the girls got back to the beach hut, having handed out Cupid Company questionnaires to anyone who looked just a little bit lonely. Coral Hut stood fresh and pretty in its new coat of pale pink, lemon-yellow and minty-green stripes. There was no other hut quite like it among those dotted along Sunday Harbour's promenade. The girls slowed to admire it.

The glossy red hut on the right-hand side of Coral Hut stood locked up tight, silent and gleaming in the bright sunlight.

The hut on the other side – named Headquarters – was painted a khaki colour and had camouflage netting thrown across its roof. Unlike the red hut, this hut buzzed with activity. Its small double doors were thrown wide open and Coral and Nicks's neighbour Birdie, was lifting and bending and packing things into a rucksack at a frantic pace.

"Are you off somewhere?" Coral called out.

"Oh, hello, dears," Birdie called over. "The Captain and I are going away for a few weeks."

The girls stood still, waiting for Birdie to say something else. Birdie was the most talkative woman they knew – she spoke in chapters, not sentences. You never had to ask Birdie for more information, but this morning she was pretty quiet.

"So where are you going to?" Nicks finally asked, when they could wait no longer.

Birdie now held a torch in her hand. She shook it irritably and pressed the on/off switch several times. Pressing her eye to the end of the torch, she tried again. This time a bright beam of yellow light shot straight out. She dropped the torch and blinked a few times, momentarily blinded.

"Er, what was that, girls?"

"Where are you going?" repeated Nicks.

Birdie retrieved the torch from the deck and placed it in a small cardboard box. "My sister has just moved up north to the city. We promised we'd visit," she finally replied.

"That is nice," said Nicks, when it was obvious that Birdie was only telling the story in very small doses.

Birdie sighed. "Not really. I'm not fond of over-populated spaces." She tried to smile – perhaps at the thought of seeing her sister – but the smile quickly dissolved into a grimace. Coral changed the subject.

"Birdie, we've been hearing some very

strange noises—" she started.

"It's terribly noisy in the city!" snorted Birdie.

Coral paused and chewed on her lip for a moment. "Not in the city... from the red beach hut next door. It sounds like—"

"Sounds like cars honking, engines roaring... traffic and trains... that's all you hear in the city," Birdie continued, ignoring them and visibly distressed. "It's not like Sunday Harbour, where everything is quiet and peaceful."

Coral decided to give it one more try. "But the noises coming from the red beach hut next door... they seem quite sinister."

"Yes, yes, I know. And you're quite right," replied Birdie. "I must brave the city for my sister." She paused and her eyes glazed over as she stared into the distance. Then she shuddered and snapped out of the moment before quickly resuming her packing. A compass, a pair of binoculars, mosquito nets, a set of two-way radios – they all went in her rucksack.

The girls watched her and sucked on their lips in concern.

"Maybe you're misjudging the city a little?" suggested Nicks when Birdie added a tray of camouflage face paint to the bag.

Birdie glanced from the bag to the girls and back again. She stood upright and gave a small chuckle. "Perhaps you're right."

Both girls sighed with relief. That was more like the old Birdie.

"Attention, please!"

The girls spun round and found their noses touching an olive-green shirt with the word ARMY spelled in black across its front. It was Birdie's husband.

"Morning, Captain!" They saluted half-heartedly (they still felt a little silly doing the salute thing).

The Captain smiled and tapped their heads affectionately. He moved over to the rucksack, limping slightly as he moved. If it weren't for his bad knee he'd still be leopard-crawling through the bush with the rest of his beloved army comrades.

"Do we have everything?" he asked.

Birdie nodded. "It should be safe to leave the rest, I think."

The Captain made a noise like a light aircraft coming in to land, as if he was considering things. "Well, I hope so," he finally replied. "And I hope we can trust those four girls to be careful with Headquarters."

"What four girls?" asked Coral, looking around Birdie and the Captain's beach hut.

Suddenly, Romeo barked. A bold seagull had landed on the deck railing behind Birdie.

"Oh, I'm sorry, girls!" said Birdie, as if Romeo had been barking directly at her. "I should have told you that my niece Saffron is going to be staying in our house while we're away. It's the least we can do – after all, she's given up her bedroom in the city for us." Just the mention of the word 'city' seemed to turn Birdie nervous again. But then she coughed hard and squared her shoulders.

"Anyway, dears, Saffron and her friends will be making use of our home and our lovely beach hut while we're away, which of course we're delighted about. We trust her completely."

The Captain made that light aircraft sort of a noise again. "Out of sight, out of mind, I say," he replied. "We can't take any chances with my specialised army gear." He glanced lovingly at the rucksack they were taking away with them.

Birdie rolled her eyes and bent to zip up the bag. It was clearly time for them to leave. She kissed both girls on the forehead while the Captain closed and locked the doors to Headquarters. They waved goodbye. And then they were gone...

The crashing of the waves on the beach suddenly seemed louder than they ever had before as the girls watched their friendly neighbours head off down the path.

♥ ♥

21

They stared at each other without speaking. There was no need. They'd been best friends for so long their conversations didn't always need words.

What a time for Birdie and the Captain to leave. Just when we were getting to grips with the strangeness of the hut next door.

Coral glanced down at Romeo. Of course she'd never swap her beloved pup, but if only he was just a little big bigger... with bigger teeth... and maybe a really big scary growl...

heart attack

Nicks didn't want to think about the mysterious red hut any more. And now that Birdie and the Captain had finally disappeared down the path it was time to get on with Cupid Company business. She tapped her glitter pen against her foil butterfly clipboard. "You're staring again," she said to Coral.

Coral tore her eyes away from the hut next door and bit the end of her pencil, which was actually a red plastic heart on a spring that jiggled when she wrote. At that moment she had nothing to write. There really wasn't a lot to write about. Coral stared at her blank notebook and tried to look thoughtful. And then her brain circuits lit up like a neon billboard.

"I know – we could matchmake your mum!" she called out excitedly. "She's been single since like *forever*...!"

"Well, only since she divorced my dad," Nicks said doubtfully.

But already Coral's head was flooded with good ideas. There was Mr McLeod from Arts and Crafts World (there wasn't enough pocket money in the world to buy all their beautiful beads, but family discounts would certainly help). And there was a very good chance that Frank who owned The Frozen Cow was unattached. Their choc-fudge-brownie frozen yoghurt was the best in Sunday Harbour.

"Look, forget it!" said Nicks before Coral

even had time to fully consider the man with the moustache who worked behind the counter at the surf clothing shop. "Mum doesn't want to be matchmade."

But there wasn't time for further discussion as, just then, Romeo streaked up the deck stairs like a white and caramel blur. He screeched to a halt and stood panting through his nostrils, his mouth filled with half a sandwich. A salami slice slipped out of the side in slow motion and landed on the deck with a *splat*. Romeo kept his chin raised but monitored the fallen salami with one eye. Doggy drool dripped from his lips, but he didn't budge.

"You've got it now, so you may as well eat it!" ordered Coral crossly. She had told him so many times before not to take food from people's beach picnics. Still, one piece of salami probably wouldn't do any harm.

Nicks giggled. "Maybe we should find Romeo a doggy girlfriend. It might just keep him out of trouble."

Coral made a pooh-pooh sort of face. She puckered up her lips and rubbed Romeo tenderly on his chin, which was now mucky with mayonnaise.

The girls were so busy concentrating on Romeo that they'd failed to notice that the red hut next door was slowly coming to life behind their backs.

"Ew, look at your fingers," said Nicks.

"What's wrong with them?" Coral loved her pup, drool, mayonnaise and all.

"They could do with a good wash," laughed Nicks.

"Oh, I'll just wipe them on—"

The sound of rattling keys ended Coral's sentence. Both girls spun in the direction of the sound.

There stood a very tall man – so tall his head loomed over the door frame of the red hut. And he was as thin as he was tall – so thin that the Adam's apple in his neck stood out like a second (and only slightly smaller) head. He looked like a long thin snake that had just eaten something quite large. The lump pulsed up and down like it was still alive.

Both girls sucked on the air so hard it sounded like they'd been winded.

"What a scary kind of guy..." wheezed Coral breathlessly.

Scary-kind-of-guy heard their gasps and twisted his heads left. His eyes were small and round and so dark that they seemed to reach out and hook on to the girls. They couldn't have looked away if they'd tried. The black pinpoints of his eyes drilled into theirs like a locked-on laser beam. And still the lump in his neck pulsed. Up-down. Up-down. Up-down.

Forever came and went and still they all stared at each other. And then, suddenly, Scary Guy moved the long thin sticks of his fingers. The keys on the round brass ring in his left hand banged together, the sound echoing like the *clang* of a giant brass bell. It even seemed to surprise Scary Guy, who all of sudden dropped the brown leather bag he'd been carrying. It landed with a monumental *thud*. The impact of the fall sprang the lock and the two halves of the bag suddenly split apart and fell wide open. They all stared at the bag as its contents spilled out across the decking. There was a hammer, a long coil of rope and a roll of thick silver duct tape.

Suddenly, Scary Guy stooped low, and in no more than two swift movements he had scooped the lot back up into the bag and snapped it shut. He was just as quick to unlock the hut's door and disappear inside, slamming the door shut behind him.

And then the world seemed especially quiet. A wind came up and blew the girls' hair, but still they didn't move. They were all big eyes and thumping chests. It was Romeo's howl that finally broke the spell. It was almost as though he sensed that something was up.

Coral was the first to breathe again. "Wow wee…" she gasped. "What do you make of that?"

28

Nicks was the first to actually move again. She slithered on to a deckchair and tapped her knees thoughtfully. "He was a strange one," she said. "Did you see the stuff in his bag?"

Coral nodded solemnly. "You do know what the most common use for duct tape is, don't you?"

Nicks shrugged lightly. If Coral was going into crazy mode there was no point in encouraging her.

"Kidnapping... murder... that sort of thing!" Coral cried out, grabbing the air with her hands and giving it a good shake.

Now it was Nicks's turns to snort, only she made more of a delicate *pssht* sort of sound. "Oh, please, where do you get that from?"

"I watch television! Where there's dodgy business – there's duct tape. No criminal can be without it."

"Keep your voice down." Nicks glanced left, then right, before whispering, "So you're suggesting that our neighbour is a criminal?"

Coral paused and took a deep breath. "Not just a criminal. A—" She stopped herself. Actually, she wasn't exactly sure what she was suggesting. But she was convinced that Scary Guy was up to no good. Why else did you carry duct tape, a hammer and rope around with you?

Coral did an about-turn and tiptoed inside Coral Hut. She really needed to lie down on the lovely bright white daybed for a bit. She wanted to rest and think the whole dramatic incident through.

Coral sighed as she absorbed it all. She felt better already. Almost. Sort of. With just a bit more rest...

queen of hearts

Nicks and her mum were still jumping the early-morning waves the next day as Coral made her way over to the beach hut, feeling queasy from all the saltwater she'd swallowed. She climbed up the front steps and settled down on her beach towel, pressing her tummy to the deck, and resting her chin on her hands at the edge. The view was good and the warm morning sun had turned the deck toasty. She could even see the top of Romeo's snoozing head poking out of the cool hole he'd dug in the warming sand. And then, very slowly, she started dozing off. When suddenly—

"SAY IT ISN'T SO!"

The voice was so loud. Coral hoisted one eye up.

"I don't even know what that colour is!"

"It's called khaki."

"They should call it KAK-i instead."

"Oh dear."

"And what's that hanging over the roof?"

"It's camouflage netting – my uncle's ex-army." This particular voice sounded weary.

Coral raised the other eyelid ever so slowly. The image of four older girls came into focus. They were standing in front of Headquarters with lipglossed lips and manicured fingers pinching their trim hips. They all wore variations of the same sort of thing: bikinis, knotted sarongs, oversized sunglasses, wide-brimmed sunhats, and enormous beach bags dangling from the crooks of their bent arms. They looked like a fashion shoot. Coral guessed they must be about eighteen years old. She kept her eyes half-mast and watched them carefully.

"We could spruce the place up a bit?" suggested the weary voice with forced cheeriness. "I'm sure my aunt and uncle won't mind if we add our own pretty touches."

So that was Saffron – Birdie and the Captain's niece. Coral zoned in on her – with her sequined clothes, shimmering glass-bead accessories and glittery lipgloss, she was obviously a sparkly sort of girl.

"We'd have to do a lot to pretty this place up!" muttered a girl with long, dark red hair.

"Oh, Tallulah, don't be such a bore," ordered a girl with wavy blonde hair. "Do you remember our last makeover? Now did we transform that girl from drab to fab?"

Tallulah gave this some thought. And then

she smiled. "You're so right, Sienna, sweetie. We can make anything look beautiful!"

Coral was still watching carefully; she was keeping a tally too. So there was sparkly Saffron. And Tallulah the redhead and Sienna with wavy blonde hair. That just left a girl with short feathery hair who seemed preoccupied with her shoes. She pulled one leg and then tried to pull the other. But her feet were stuck fast. She seemed to think about this for a moment, then she slid her feet out of the shoes. Bending low and using both hands, she yanked the shoes from the sand. She'd worn high heels to the beach!

Saffron already had the double doors of Headquarters pulled wide open. She was surveying the interior of the hut with her enormous beach bag still dangling from her arm while she tapped a fingernail against her front teeth. She seemed to be thinking out loud.

"Some glittery dangly decorations... a

34

crystal bead curtain, perhaps… flowers… a few scented tea candles…"

The other two girls – Tallulah and Sienna – had also taken an interest in the hut. Tallulah was testing the spring of the army cot bed with her bouncing bottom (except there was not much bouncing to be done). She looked less than impressed with the hard mattress. She muttered something about "So much for comfy afternoon naps," while Sienna turned the Captain's brass bugle this way and that in her hands. She then put the bugle to her eye and looked through it like a telescope. She seemed less than impressed too.

Saffron meanwhile was humming a tune while she busily dressed one of the beach hut's windows in her (unsurprisingly) sparkly sarong. After a few minor adjustments to the sarong tassels she stepped back to admire her decorating. At last somebody looked pleased.

"Time to suntan!" squealed the girl who was now sensibly carrying the high heels in her hand. She had found a spot on the sand directly in front of Headquarters, and was dropping everything – a large pink towel, a glossy magazine, various bottles (suntan oil, sunblock, cooling mist face spray, mineral water) and her mobile phone. She then finally settled down on her towel with the magazine and began to read out loud.

"How do you know if you're loved up?" she demanded.

Coral's ears pricked up.

"You have to answer A, B or C," the girl finished.

The other girls stopped what they were doing and nodded thoughtfully.

"Question one," the girl went on. "It's your first-year anniversary and your boyfriend: a) buys you flowers and choccies or b) makes you a card or c) gives you an extra special cuddle because it's not about gifts anyway?"

The rest of the girls were silent. Tallulah was the first to speak. "Is there a D, Chanel?"

Ah, so that was the girl's name, thought Coral.

"I told you there's only A, B or C," Chanel went on.

"Are they fancy florist flowers or flowers bought from the local petrol station?" asked Saffron.

Coral could barely stifle a snigger.

"I think a handmade card is very sweet. I'd say B," decided Sienna.

"Cuddle – I'd choose an extra special cuddle," replied Tallulah, who had obviously given up on the non-existent D option.

Chanel sat upright and grinned happily at her friends. "Isn't it just brilliant that we all have boyfriends!"

Coral groaned inwardly. So no matchmaking to be had here then.

"Having a boyfriend just makes the world seem brighter," Saffron agreed. "Even if I'm having a bad day I just have to think about Max and suddenly I feel better." She hugged herself and smiled in a warm and cosy sort of way.

Chanel nodded. "That's the power of love. Having a love life is just the best! But it's good that we still have time for our girlfriends too."

The other girls all nodded and started talking at once.

"Right on, sister!"

"Of course we miss the boys."

"But they'll still be there when we get back from our holiday!"

"Here's to girl power!"

"And the power of love!"

Coral stared awestruck at her shiny and sophisticated new neighbours. You really didn't get girls like these in Sunday Harbour. These big-city girls looked and behaved like film stars. And they seemed to love 'love' just as much as Coral and Nicks did!

Suddenly, a cool wind sprang up and goosebumps popped up on Coral's skin. She needed to get dressed. But she didn't want to draw attention to herself – not in her plain old boring school swimming costume anyway. It had been at the top of the laundry pile and had made for easy grabbing. She scowled at her laziness. Of course she couldn't wait to meet her fabulous new neighbours, but she wanted to make the best first impression too. So there was nothing else for her to do but slowly leopard crawl backwards along the deck in the direction of the door to Coral Hut. Along the way she stubbed her toe on a deckchair and scraped a knee on the bare deckboards, but it was worth it. She made it inside the hut without being noticed.

Her purple and pink heart-shaped backpack was still on the daybed and she zipped it open. All she'd brought with her was a hooded top, a pair of board shorts printed with yellow smiling starfish and her Crocs. It was hardly an outfit torn from the pages of a magazine, but it was all she had. She sighed and put on everything except for the Crocs. She was now as ready as she could be for her grand entrance.

She tiptoed back to the doorway for one more inspection. Her timing had to be perfect. She carefully put her nose round the corner. She glanced right. The girls were reading magazines, filing their nails and nattering. She glanced left. *SCARY GUY WAS ON THE DECK OF THE RED HUT AND STARING DIRECTLY AT HER!*

Coral screamed.

The big-city girls over at Headquarters screamed too (Coral's scream had just given them the biggest fright).

Scary Guy quickly disappeared through the door of the glossy red hut and snapped it shut behind him again.

Nobody else moved. Coral stood still, framed in the doorway, her breathing slowing again. The girls were all staring at her. She hoisted up her eyebrows in an innocent sort of way, then gave a small whistle before tucking her hands inside her pockets. Or she tried to, anyway. As it turned out this particular pair of board shorts didn't have any pockets, so she had to cross her arms instead.

Sienna was fanning her face with a nail file while Tallulah pressed her magazine against her chest. Finally Saffron spoke.

"Is everything all right, little girl?"

Little girl? Coral glanced around before she realised that they must be referring to her.

She coughed. "Oh yes. Oh, sure," she replied as she stumbled out on to the deck. OK, so it wasn't quite the grand entrance she'd planned.

"Have you hurt yourself?" asked Chanel, who was now nervously clutching her sunhat.

Coral shook her head.

"Did something scare you then?" asked Sienna with a sad face, like Coral was five years old and the bogey man had suddenly appeared from under the bed.

"Scare me?" she spluttered. "Definitely not." She hadn't got a plan, or time to come up with one either. But the girls were all staring and waiting expectantly. So she suddenly let out another scream. And then she grinned and shrugged. "When I'm really happy I just sometimes give a good scream." She smiled sweetly.

The girls seemed to be thinking about this for a moment before slowly starting to move about again. Sienna resumed nail filing and Chanel put her sunhat back on.

"So happy I could scream..." said Tallulah with her head tilted left then right. "Yes, I think I've heard that saying before."

Sienna nodded while she filed. "It does sound very familiar."

"Aaaah!" screamed Chanel.

Saffron echoed her scream and then so did the other two girls. They all grinned at each other. Coral grinned at the girls. They grinned back. There was a lot of crazy grinning. Coral could see she was going to like these girls a lot.

from the heart

The four girls had already disappeared off to explore the sights and sounds of Sunday Harbour when Nicks got back – pale and puckered – from her wave-jumping session. Coral didn't mention the arrival of the fabulous, big-city girls next door. She simply locked Coral Hut and, with her best friend and her puppy on either side of her, smiled quietly before leaving for home. Not that there was any big hurry. The sun was still high in the sky and lunchtime was a safe distance away, so the two girls ambled along slowly and spoke even less.

Nicks's cheeks had been painted pink by the sunshine; Coral's glowed with happiness from her small sweet secret. Nicks was quiet because she was tired; whereas Coral was keeping silent as she wanted to savour the girls' glitzy glamour (without interruption) for just a little while longer. She had a suspicion that Nicks might not be quite as impressed by the lipglossed, lovestruck ways of the four big-city girls as she was. Nicks was a much more sensible sort.

The trio were just strolling past the Seafood Shack when Romeo stopped. His black nose sniffed the air hungrily, but the girls kept on walking. They passed the bakery, but still the girls kept on walking. It was only when they came to the local charity shop that Coral slowed and came to a standstill.

"Come on, I'm bushed," groaned Nicks, who was now a short distance ahead.

Coral's nose was flattened against the shop's window. "Oh, you have to see this!" She jabbed a finger at the glass and tapped it excitedly.

Nicks knew there was no point in resisting, so she trudged over to see what the fuss was about. Beyond the glass window pane were a pair of used ski boots and a set of four teacups with an uneven number of saucers. Neither of those could be what had got Coral so excited. And then Nicks noticed the mannequin with the missing arm that was half hidden by a bright pink feather boa. Now that was just Coral's sort of thing.

"It's pretty, but where would you even wear a pink feather boa?" she said.

"No, not the feather boa. Look!" Coral jabbed her finger at the glass a few more times.

And then Nicks noticed the square brown cardboard box with the words VALENTINE PARTY DECORATIONS (Going Cheap!) scrawled

45

and underlined in thick blue marker pen across one side.

"Could we do this another time?" Nicks suggested half-heartedly.

But Coral had a determined grin on her face. "No way – it'll be snapped up before we know it!"

"But we're months away from Valentine's Day," Nicks groaned.

But Coral wasn't listening. "A box full of romance!" she sighed blissfully. "C'mon, I have pocket money." And then she disappeared through the charity shop's door.

Nicks hesitated for a moment before scooping Romeo up in her arms and following her friend inside. She found Coral pointing at the box in the window, already discussing her potential purchase with the grey-haired lady behind the till.

"Oh, I remember the poor young dear who donated that box of Valentine decorations to the shop. I remember her well," she was saying.

"That girl sobbed her heart out right on the spot where you're standing now. You see, she'd just lost her one great love."

Nicks watched Coral. She was rooted to the spot and staring, silent and unmoving. Her lower lip looked ready to tremble.

"But *how* did she lose her one great love?" Coral cried out, her mind was reviewing all the possibilities. Was it an illness? An accident? Some natural disaster?

"He ran off with the blonde from Belarus," replied the charity shop lady matter-of-factly.

Coral's concentrated face of emotion dissolved instantly. "Oh right," she said. It was hardly the epic love story she'd been hoping for.

"And the young girl said she never wanted to celebrate Valentine's Day ever again," concluded the lady, like she had come to the unhappily-ever-after end of the story.

Coral thought about the dumped girl. If only they knew who she was. There was no doubt in Coral's mind that the Cupid Company could help her to find love once again.

"So will you be buying the box of decorations in the window?" the lady asked.

Nicks already knew Coral's answer. "I'll fetch it," she quickly answered. She really just wanted to get home.

She returned carrying the box, but Coral couldn't wait for home. Already she was dipping both hands excitedly into the tangle of decorations dedicated to love. The air was instantly a flurry of red and pink and silver. There were padded fabric hearts that said FOREVER, BE MINE and LOVE BUG. There were dangling cupids, foil garlands of red and silver hearts, heart-shaped window stickers, balloons that spelled L FOR LOVE and a banner that said I LOVE YOU. There was even a tub of fake rose petals for scattering. Coral sighed noisily and stared, starry-eyed. She was in Coral Heaven. And then she thought about the girl whose boyfriend had run off with the blonde from

Belarus. It was like holding a piece of history. She sighed again, but was soon drawn to the other items in the charity shop, which was like an Aladdin's Cave of treasures. Her hands reached for the overflowing shelves, railings and baskets.

"Give the lady your money, Coral," ordered Nicks.

But Coral had already found another treasure.

"Coral!" A tired Nicks was getting impatient.

Coral spun round with a giant pair of oversized tortoiseshell sunglasses on her nose.

"Ha ha, very funny," said Nicks. "But I'm really in no mood for fooling about." She gripped the wriggling Romeo even closer.

"Who's fooling about?" grinned Coral as she flounced in the direction of a basket of discounted scarves. Dipping her hands inside, she let her fingers ripple through the soft and silky material. Of course she knew there wasn't much time left ticking on her best friend's meter, but she hardly needed any time at all. Quickly she found what she was looking for and held it up, smiling. The grey animal-print silk scarf with the sparkle stripe was very fashionable.

Nicks was huffing and puffing now and tapping her foot impatiently, but she clearly wasn't quite ready to expire just yet. So Coral took one last dip into the basket and came up with a purple paisley bandanna. It would be perfect for Romeo. She gave a small joyful whoop and carried her final purchases over to the till where her box of Valentine decorations was still waiting. This had been her best shopping day ever!

The lady accepted Coral's money with a gentle smile and was about to place the sunglasses, the scarf and the bandanna inside the box of decorations for easy carrying when Coral slipped the sunglasses from her grip and returned her smile.

"Thanks very much," she said, "but I'll be

needing those." She put the sunglasses on her nose and pushed them up as far as they would go. "C'mon, Nicks. C'mon, Romeo." And then she swished out of the shop with the box of decorations hoisted under one arm like a very big trophy.

Nicks hurried after her, relieved to be leaving, but also a little confused by the sunglasses (although her best friend did have a strange sense of humour). Coral was outside and waiting on the pavement, still wearing the oversized glasses.

"Don't you think you should take those things off now?" asked Nicks.

"Take them off? Whatever for?"

"Oh, please, stop being silly."

"I am not being silly. All the celebs wear these. We'll need to find you a pair too."

Nicks groaned and made a choking sort of sound. "I don't think so. They don't even fit you properly."

Coral tilted her head at a backwards angle

and started walking, narrowly missing a large lamppost.

Nicks returned Romeo to the pavement and quickly caught up with her zigzagging friend. She was no longer feeling quite so tired.

"So how are the sunglasses working out for you then?" she asked with a smirk that was almost as big as her friend's sunglasses.

"Great!" Coral looked awkward but determined. "They're lovely," she said, almost smacking straight into a postbox. She held on to the box of Valentine decorations even tighter. Nicks decided it was wiser not to even ask what she planned to do with those. It looked like her best friend just needed to focus all of her concentration on getting home safely!

heartland

Coral had got Nicks to promise she would be at her house at nine the next morning, and now Coral was counting on it – literally. There was a small clock on her bedside table that she was watching, its two heart-shaped hands edging forward.

"Coral, Nicks is here!" her mum called up from the kitchen.

"Send her to my bedroom, please!" Coral hollered back.

"Must you all shout to one another?" her father called from the study.

"Sorry!" both Coral and her mum cried in unison.

And then Nicks's head appeared round the bedroom door. "Wowzers," she breathed out loud.

"Isn't it brilliant!" Coral grinned.

Nicks stepped inside the bedroom. There were pink padded hearts tied with ribbon to cupboard handles, lamps and the bed frame. The ceiling was alive with swirling hearts and dangling cupids. The banner across the wall above her bed spelled out: I LOVE YOU and strings of red and silver foiled hearts dipped from corner to corner. There were even bunches of balloons tied to the bedposts and red hearts stuck to the windows. The finishing touch was the fake rose petals scattered across the carpet. Nicks swished through them like autumn leaves, noticing Romeo's face poking out from under the bed.

"It's certainly very Valentiney," Nicks commented. Even if it wasn't that time of year. But she didn't say the last bit out loud.

"It's a room dedicated to love and romance," said Coral excitedly. "Can you think of anything nicer!" It wasn't a question, and Nicks knew better than to answer.

Nicks gazed around the room with her hands on her hips and grinned. "It is lovely!"

Coral reached for her heart-shaped backpack and pulled out the giant tortoiseshell sunglasses. "Shall we get going then? Romeo could do with a paddle in the sea. It's going to be a hot one."

"Sure." Nicks patted her knees to encourage Romeo out from under the bed. He crawled slowly forward. He was not his usual hyperactive self – perhaps because he had a purple paisley bandanna tied like a loose scarf around his neck!

Coral spied the bandanna and clucked loudly. "I almost forgot!" She reached for the animal-print silk scarf with the sparkle stripe running through it and draped it round her own neck.

"Right, are we all ready then?" she said brightly.

Nicks stared at the scarf thoughtfully. "It would seem so," she finally replied. She'd known Coral to have crazy turns before (although this was a new kind of crazy). But time and experience had taught her that sometimes saying or doing nothing at all was by far the quicker route to getting things back to normal again.

It took them a bit longer than usual to reach the beach hut because Coral was still forced to walk with her head tilted at a backwards angle to avoid the oversized sunglasses slipping down her nose. And when they finally arrived at the hut, it was at almost exactly the same time as their new big-city neighbours.

Coral spied the four older girls and her mouth pulled wide with a grin shaped like a crescent moon. She fiddled with the scarf

round her neck and practised saying the girls'
names under her breath: "Hi, Saffron. Hi,
Sienna. Hi, Tallulah. Hi, Chanel."

"Who are those girls?" Nicks asked.

"The girl with the sparkle top is Birdie and
the Captain's niece – she's called Saffron. The
rest of the girls are her friends," replied Coral
authoritatively. "We met yesterday." She
thought about this for a moment, and then
realised that they actually hadn't met the day
before – or not officially anyway. She only knew
their names because she'd sort of been
eavesdropping. And they didn't know her name
either. "Well, we *sort of* met yesterday," she
finally added as she stumbled her way up the
deck steps. She was quite relieved to be in the
shade of the beach hut again: it gave her a good
reason to remove the sunglasses. Her neck was
beginning to ache.

As Nicks opened Coral Hut, she found a
brand-new completed Cupid Company questionnaire
slipped beneath the door. Transporting it inside

like it was hidden treasure, she sat down on the daybed to read it through carefully. Only then would she be able to compare it to the other questionnaires on their files and decide if they might or might not have a good match.

Coral meanwhile pulled up a deck chair, angling it so that it was close to the deck railings with a good – but not obviously direct – view of the girls next door. She then returned the oversized sunglasses to her nose and settled back into the chair to watch and learn.

There was some nail painting going on and Sienna seemed to be practising a French braid in Tallulah's hair. Chanel was holding a round mirror up to her face, seemingly exfoliating her lips with a small brush. Coral watched, fascinated. Where was Saffron? And then suddenly there she was, carrying a plant under each arm. One had red flowers; the other was bright yellow. Lovingly, she placed the pretty pots beside the other colourful pot plants that now nestled together beneath the windows of

Headquarters. She'd obviously been working hard all morning, and the hut was already transformed by the beautiful blossoms.

Just then a mobile phone beeped. All four girls leaped into action, digging frantically in pockets or scrambling madly for their beach bags. Finally, a victorious Tallulah held her mobile phone high in the air. "It's mine!" she announced gleefully before turning her attention to the phone's screen. "And it's from Ethan. Aw. And he says he's missing me!"

All four girls tilted their heads to one side and released a collective "aaah" sound into the air.

"He really does love you," crooned Chanel.

"Oh, ta, Chanel," replied Tallulah. "And Tyler loves you so much too."

Both girls tilted their heads to one side and gave another "aaah" sound like their boyfriends were the sweetest things on earth.

"Sam still hasn't said that he loves me," grumbled Sienna with a lipglossed pout. She stared into the distance and tapped her mobile phone (which she still gripped very tightly just in case).

"I'm sure he will – very very soon," replied Chanel.

"Yes, I wonder if these boys know how lucky they are to have such fabulous girlfriends," added Saffron with a giggle. The rest of her friends laughed along with her.

"We were right to leave them at home and take this girly holiday, weren't we?" said Sienna, a nervous frown pressing lines in her forehead.

Tallulah nodded passionately. "Of course! I mean, they're probably just sitting at home missing us. Right?"

"Definitely," agreed Chanel. And then she seemed to be thinking about it some more. She no longer looked as sure as she'd sounded. But then she shook her head and gave a firm nod, like she was determined not to be silly. "We've got to trust in true love. They probably can't wait for us to get home," she added with a delicate chuckle. The rest of her friends chuckled along with her. They did like to do things together.

Coral watched and listened and almost chuckled, but stopped herself just in time.

"Hey, girls, move in closer," said Tallulah in a sort of hushed whisper. The girls instantly shuffled nearer to their redhead friend. "Before we left for our holiday Ethan said that…"

And then her whisper faded completely. Coral leaned as close as she could. She even angled her head so that her ears could cup any passing words carried along by the sea breeze. But still she couldn't catch another word spoken by Tallulah. She'd have needed superhuman eardrums for that.

So she stood up from her deck chair, stretched and yawned, and leaned over the railings. Resting her elbows on the edge, she admired the view with her ears sticking out like two satellite dishes. But she still couldn't hear a word. Tallulah was obviously a very good whisperer. The view was a good one though. She could see the girls even better now; they were huddled together with their shoulders and heads touching.

And then they all went "OOOH!" and scattered.

Coral quickly pulled herself backwards and dropped to her haunches with her back pressed against the railings. As she sat there with her knees round her ears she wondered what she should do next. She also wondered why she was crouched there in the first place; it was hardly like it made her invisible. Thankfully no one seemed to have noticed her.

And then Nicks was standing over her. She'd obviously finished sorting through the completed questionnaires. "Coral, what are you doing on the floor?"

Coral rose slowly and leaned casually against the railings. "Just inspecting the deck and checking that it's still sturdy, you know –

general maintenance..."

"Hey look, it's that girl who screams when she's happy!" Saffron called out as she pointed at Coral. She then followed this with a small, elegant scream of her own.

The other girls all grinned and also tossed their own delicate screams into the sea breeze.

Nicks stood there with her hands on her hips and a small frown perched between her eyes. Coral turned slightly pink and shrugged, like *What other choice do I have?* And then she hung her own high-pitched happy scream on the salty air.

heartbreak

"So what are your names?" asked Saffron once all the screams had faded. She smiled at Coral and Nicks sweetly, like *Aren't they just the cutest!*

Nicks's hands were still perched on her hips and her frown deepened. Coral still had a grin stuck to her face.

"My name is Nicks," Nicks finally said. "And this is my friend and business associate, Coral."

Her voice sounded deeper than usual. She did sound very grown-up. Coral's grin stretched wider as she raised a hand in the air and flapped it about like a fish.

"Nicks and Coral," Saffron repeated. "What pretty names. And you're *business* associates too. Mmm." She turned to her friends and made big eyes that said: *Couldn't you just eat them up!*

Nicks's gaze narrowed. Coral still grinned. "Yes, and this is our hut. It's called Coral Hut," she called out excitedly. She felt sure that the older girls would be mightily impressed by the fact that the hut was named after her. Sort of.

"It's such a pretty hut," said Tallulah admiringly. "Did you choose the colour scheme?"

Coral nodded so enthusiastically she almost dislodged a neck vertebra. "Oh yes! It's definitely our... uh... design." The truth lay like an obstacle course before her. So she was ducking and diving a bit, but they had played a very big part in decorating the outside of their hut (even if her father had bought the colours on sale and their friend Jake had directed the stripes). "And this is my pup Romeo," she suddenly added in a flash of inspiration. She was pulling out all the big guns, desperately wanting to impress the older girls any and every which way.

"Oooh," the girls crooned with their shiny lips pouted. But Romeo barely even glanced up from his snooze on the deck chair. He'd already scoped out the menu next door; rice cakes and mineral water did not interest him.

Coral couldn't wait to tell the girls about the Cupid Company – she was sure it would impress them more than anything. But their neighbourly conversation ended just as suddenly as it had begun.

"Right, well I've got a suntan to work on," announced Chanel. "Nice chatting to you girlies."

The other girls obviously had suntans to

work on too because they all scattered with a brief "Bye bye" and a "See you soon" and quickly busied themselves applying suntan lotion and sunhats. Nicks gave a polite farewell nod while Coral flapped her hand in the air for a second time that morning. Only this time the flapping was less energetic. She had so hoped to tell them about the Cupid Company. But worst of all was that she'd forgotten to ask the girls their names. Of course she already *knew* their names. But the girls didn't know this. Perhaps they thought that Coral and Nicks didn't care enough to ask. And Coral cared very much.

"Right then." Nicks exhaled deeply and finally smiled. "Down to business. Harry, who runs the Beach Huts Association, slipped a completed Cupid Company questionnaire beneath Coral Hut's door." She did look pleased.

Coral thought about Harry and sighed half-heartedly. "Harry. Yes, he's nice."

67

"Yes he is," agreed Nicks. "And now we have to find someone nice to introduce him to... mmm." She tapped her foil butterfly clipboard thoughtfully while she paged through the other completed questionnaires they had on file.

The older girls on the patch of sand in front of Headquarters were lying flat on their backs while Sienna sat propped up against her giant beach bag and read out loud from her magazine. Coral strained to hear – it sounded like Sienna had the latest romance horoscopes in hand.

"What about the Russian girl Zinaida who works at the Seaside Store?" suggested Nicks.

"What about her?" mumbled a distracted Coral. Had she overheard correctly? Were Aquarians and Scorpios a love match made in heaven?

"You know – for Harry?"

Just then one of the mobile phones on the patch of sand in front of Headquarters beeped loudly with a text message. And just like before, the girls reacted like they'd been collectively stung by jellyfish – squealing and moving very quickly. They grabbed their phones and rapidly checked their screens. This time it was Sienna who held her phone up in the air victoriously.

"It's mine!" she cried happily. "It's Sam." And then she put her nose down and scrolled through the message. At first her painted finger pressed the scroll-down button quickly. But then it slowed.

"I bet he's missing you," cooed Chanel.

"I bet he's begging her to come home early," tittered Saffron.

Finally Sienna stopped scrolling and glanced around at her friends. For a few endless moments she remained quiet. And then she gave a loud (less than ladylike) wail. "SAM HAS JUST DUMPED ME BY TEXT!"

The rest of the girls sat there, stunned. And then they gasped as a group. "Never!"

Whether this was because she'd been dumped, or dumped by text, was difficult to tell.

Sienna was now sobbing so much she could barely speak. "He says. It's not me. It's him. And some other girl. He said. I would have found out. Eventually," she managed between sobs and hiccups. "And. This girl. She's a... football supporter!" she cried out, howling so loudly Romeo jumped up and wiggled his ears. His doggy instincts were on red alert.

"A football supporter!" echoed her friends with delicate wrinkled noses. Even Nicks watched closely. Being a boyfriend thief obviously did not earn the respect of these girls. And being dumped for a thieving boyfriend football supporter seemed to be the most horrendous news ever!

all heart

Nicks had always been a mind-your-own-business sort of girl so she tuned out quickly from the drama at Headquarters and settled back into her deck chair with Harry's questionnaire. It wasn't that she was heartless; she just wasn't the nosy type. Coral, on the other hand, found it very difficult to focus on anything else.

"So Harry likes nature walks and bird watching," revealed Nicks while she read. "He's passionate about protecting marine life, hates litter and is a devoted vegetarian. He's also added an extra page to our questionnaire, listing what lobby groups he's a member of." She turned to the page in question. "He belongs to the Beach Huts Association and the Community Alliance. He's also a long-standing member of *Save our Seaside Suburbs* and *People Against Underwater Noise Pollution*." Nicks glanced up at Coral with a thoughtful frown. "So what do you think?"

"I think dumping someone by text is just cowardly," murmured Coral with a small shake of her head. She was still staring at a blubbing Sienna. Her friends had encircled the sad girl and stood patiently tapping her hand and shoulder while they cooed thoughtful phrases like "It'll be OK" and "He'll definitely come back to you".

But Sienna didn't seem remotely interested in their gurgled reassurances. Instead, she clambered unsteadily to her feet and, with her fists raised at the heavens, cried out loudly, "I NEED DOUBLE CHOC-CHIP ICE CREAM NOW!"

The girl who had once been all bouncy blonde curls and confidence was changed. It was like her whole body had gone into meltdown. Her cheeks were already swollen and red and bisected by two thick black mascara stains. Her golden hair had lost its curl and hung limply around her now rounded, slumped shoulders. Her shiny lips had rubbed off and her pretty face was twisted and miserable.

"Of course you need ice cream!" replied the girls nervously as they immediately ushered her in the direction of Mr Gelatti's ice cream van. They seemed relieved to have something to do to take her mind off ratfink boyfriend Sam.

Coral watched them leave with a feeling of sadness. Not only was it tragic to see love crash and burn, but she felt like she was already a part of the melodrama and now the action was disappearing down the beach. She should be there. With them.

Nicks looked less sad. Of course she pitied the wailing girl who was now on the rampage heading for double chocolate-chip ice cream, but they really had Cupid Company business to attend to. She turned her attention back to the two completed questionnaires before her.

"So, Harry plays the harmonica. And it says here that Zinaida plays piano. It's great that they share a love of music," she considered out loud. "And they're both eighteen years old – so they're the same age too."

"Yes, love..." echoed Coral wistfully. Poor Sienna. The older girls were already quite a distance along the beach, but Coral could still make out Sienna's crumpled shape wedged in between the other girls.

Nicks ignored her mumbling friend and continued reading from Zinaida's questionnaire. The two girls were both lost in very different worlds. And then Coral sat ramrod straight. She cocked her head left then right as she considered the idea that had just brainstormed her head...

What about... mmm... OH YES, DEFINITELY!

"We should send Sienna on a date with Harry!" she shouted out loud.

"Who is Sienna?" Nicks asked calmly. She was quite used to her friend's wild ideas.

Coral remembered that she only knew the older girls' names from her eavesdropping. This meant that Nicks had no idea who Sienna was.

"She's the girl next door who has just been dumped by text. She's heartbroken! So it's the duty of the Cupid Company to help mend her heart and gently show love is on its way again."

Of course Coral's motives were fuelled by her love for love, but she had a smaller, sneakier reason too: matchmaking was also an excellent way to get to know the older girls better. Helping to turn Sienna's frown upside down could just secure her a prime place in their good books. She might even become a part of their group (with Nicks, of course). Already she was imagining them hanging out at Headquarters, taking *How Romantic Are You?* quizzes and nattering about boyfriends (the older girls' boyfriends, obviously).

Nicks thought about Sienna for a moment. She did feel sorry for the dumped girl, but they really knew very little more about her than that. "She'll have to fill in a questionnaire first," she said.

"Her friends will do it for her, I'm sure. Sienna is in no state to fill anything in," countered Coral protectively. She'd seen enough romantic films to know that people with broken hearts could not be expected to do anything useful – not for a while, anyway. This was exactly why they always went about in their pyjamas. She was suddenly very excited. This was her chance to help Sienna find real love (Harry was a nice guy while Sam was quite obviously a non-nice guy). And she was about to become very close friends with the glamorous girls next door.

If there were any doubts in her mind (which there weren't really), the next five seconds would change that. She reached for her tortoiseshell sunglasses, prepared to put them on her nose and then thought better of it. She balanced them on her head instead. And then Harry from the Beach Huts Association suddenly made an appearance. Fate was quite obviously in on her brilliant plan to matchmake nice-guy Harry and Sienna.

Coral grinned at the boy with glasses and a canvas bag slung across his chest. His skin looked as soft and pale as marshmallows and contrasted with the thick, sticking-up dark hair on his head. He was dressed in a Hawaiian shirt and baggy shorts in bright colours and a large, eager smile.

"Hi, Coral! Hi, Nicks!" Harry smiled.

"Hi, Harry," the girls said at once.

77

Yes, he definitely was Mr Nice, mused Coral. He was nice-*looking* too. And yet she'd never known him to have a girlfriend. He didn't hang out with the cool crowd at the beach. Unlike most of the other lads his age, it seemed like Harry was very busy with the serious business of saving things. But if Harry was a bit of a geek, he was certainly the nicest geek she knew.

"Did you receive my completed questionnaire?" he asked. "I popped it under your hut door last night." His eyebrows were raised hopefully.

"Oh yes. Thanks. I have it right here." Nicks tapped her clipboard and observed their new Cupid Company client carefully.

Harry's hands rubbed together eagerly. "So do you have a date lined up for me yet?"

"Just about!" crowed Coral. "In fact we think we have the perfect girl for you." She'd made up her mind: Mr Nice *deserved* to find love! If you didn't count Romeo, who was curled up and sleeping in a pool of sunlight, Nicks's face was the only one there that wasn't stretched wide with excitement. She felt that being a nice guy didn't necessarily make Harry well suited to Sienna. This was crazy, haphazard matchmaking and it was not her careful way of doing things. But she didn't want to have that argument with Coral in front of Harry, who looked as happy as a prizewinner.

"I'm available any time!" he confirmed with his best winning grin.

Coral just happened to glance up and over Harry's happy head to the stretch of beach behind him. Their neighbours were already on their way back from Mr Gelatti's van! You couldn't miss Sienna, who still wore the oily black mascara stains down her cheeks and seemed to be violently attacking the ice cream she carried in both hands. This was definitely not the right time for Harry to meet Sienna.

"That's good to hear, Harry," she stammered nervously. "We'll be in touch."

"When?"

"Soon."

"How soon?"

"Very soon!"

Harry mulled this over with a face that clearly wondered *Just how soon is very soon?*

"Before you know it!" added Coral forcefully.

Harry seemed to deflate right before her eyes. Even his smile shrank with a *pshht* sort of sound. Coral checked on the progress of Sienna and her friends. They were coming closer and closer.

"OK, we'll be in touch tomorrow!" she promised urgently. She turned to Nicks for confirmation, but Nicks simply crossed her arms and stared straight ahead (*If Coral had only done things my way...*)

But finally Harry nodded his surrender; it seemed that he could manage to wait one more day. And then he waved his goodbye and turned away.

Coral breathed again.

Suddenly Harry paused before turning back to the girls.

Coral stopped breathing.

"I forgot to give you this," he said as he fished inside the canvas bag slung across his chest. He pulled out a white printed leaflet that he handed to Coral, who was distracted with checking on the progress of Sienna and her friends. *The girls were so close!*

"Great! Thanks, Harry. See ya!" she said as she snatched the paper from his fingers.

Harry stared for a moment and then turned away thoughtfully. He wandered over to the glossy red beach hut and beyond, handing out leaflets or slipping them under hut doors as he went.

Coral breathed again – and then Sienna and the rest of the girls arrived back at Headquarters. The timing had been split-second. Nicks rolled her eyes, shook her head and pulled Harry's leaflet from Coral's grip.

IS YOUR BEACH HUT SOMETHING SPECIAL?

THEN ENTER THE BEACH HUTS ASSOCIATION'S

BEST BEACH HUT COMPETITION.

JUDGING TAKES PLACE SATURDAY 20th JULY

Of course Coral Hut was something special. *Of course* they would enter the Best Beach Hut competition – if only Nicks could get Coral to focus on something other than those girls next door for just one second...

heart·shaped

Coral lay awake for what seemed like a very long time that night. But she felt more confident with the morning's light. She liked to get on with things, which was why she couldn't even wait for Nicks before racing down to their beach hut that morning. Nicks would get her message; she'd understand.

Coral quickly found what she was looking for at the hut: a washed-up lump of coral shaped like a heart. She'd always really liked it and felt sure that the girls next door would like it too. After all, they seemed to love 'love' just as much as she did, so it really would make the perfect welcoming gift. It would no doubt pretty up Headquarters too. Delivering the heart-shaped coral was also the perfect reason to pay their neighbours a visit, and it was an even better conversation starter for the Cupid Company. It was a very useful little lump of coral. Proud of her most recent brilliant brainwaves, Coral felt like a useful lump of coral too. She chuckled and rocked while she waited.

Nicks arrived at the beach hut to find Coral perched on a deck chair, clutching a funny-shaped piece of coral and an empty questionnaire and giggling to herself. She seemed to be waiting for something. Or going la-la.

"Why were you in such a hurry to get to Coral Hut this morning?" she said, adding, "Is everything all right?"

Coral nodded. "Oh yes, I'm just waiting for Saffron and Sienna and the girls. And you know Harry will be here soon."

"Harry?" Nicks looked puzzled for a moment and then remembered Coral's promise from yesterday to fix him up on a date today.

She frowned. "It might have been an idea to get Sienna's questionnaire completed *before* promising Harry an introduction though. We don't even know if they're well suited."

Coral nodded uncomfortably, and then reminded herself that just because it had all gone wrong before for them it didn't mean that it would all go wrong again. Not necessarily. But Nicks wasn't done yet.

"And quite honestly, Coral, I don't think that Sienna is even going to want to meet someone new yet," she said. "She probably needs some time to get over her break-up."

That was one way of looking at it. Coral shrugged. But then again why spend weeks being miserable when you could just move onwards and upwards to better things (like Harry – the guy who cared about marine life and hated litter)? But there was no time for a debate because the older girls had just arrived next door. Sienna looked a bit better than she had done the previous day. She was manicured and made up, but the shimmering lipgloss, dangly earrings, flowery hairclips and fashion accessories seemed to hang off her like decorations on a Christmas tree. She just didn't seem her usual confident, comfortable self. She looked like she'd have preferred to be sitting somewhere dark, feeling miserable, but had been forced to get spruced up and out of the house.

"What a gorgeous day!" cried Tallulah with an excessive amount of cheeriness. She noticed Nicks and Coral on the deck of Coral Hut and gave a joyful *I'm-so-happy-I-could-scream* scream and a wave. She looked like she was putting a lot of effort into seeming jolly. The rest of her friends saw the girls too and also gave a hearty scream (all except for Sienna, of course).

Coral blushed a pale pink and gave a small scream in return. This *I'm-so-happy-I-could-scream* thing seemed to have caught on (she'd really hoped her neighbours might have moved on from it by now). But if she seemed half-hearted the other girls hadn't appeared to notice. They were already busy with other things – like opening up the beach hut and preparing for a day of lounging in the sunshine. They were very vocal about it too. The air around their beach hut vibrated with cheery comments about the *"wonderful weather!"* and *"sensational sea view!"* and *"breathtaking warm ocean breeze that makes you SO GLAD TO BE ALIVE!"*. But Sienna didn't seem to be buying any of it. "I need more ice cream," was all she said.

"But you've already had a plate of pancakes with syrup and four breakfast muffins," replied Chanel nervously. Some of the syrupy evidence was still spread across the front of Sienna's pretty embroidered blouse.

"I'm getting ice cream!" snorted Sienna, stomping off down the beach in the direction of Mr Gelatti's van. Chanel scurried after her, waving a small bag of low-fat rice cakes at her friend's uninterested back. Coral saw her moment and grabbed it – as well as the lump of heart-shaped coral and a blank questionnaire – with both hands. She then patted the oversized tortoiseshell sunglasses perched on the top of her head and stroked the animal-print scarf round her neck. Now she was ready to speak to the girls!

"Hello?" she called out as she made her way over to the khaki-painted hut and climbed the steps to the deck with her sunglasses still perched on top of her head. She found Saffron inside the hut hanging a string of pink silk flowers across the Captain's green metal utility cupboard while Tallulah scooped scented potpourri into an upturned combat helmet.

Saffron noticed their visitor first.

"Hey, Nicks," she said.

"It's Coral."

Saffron stared down at the lump in the younger girl's hands and nodded. "Yes, I think you're right."

"No, I mean I'm Coral."

Saffron's face broke with a smile. "Of course you are. Sorry. And I'm Saffron."

"And I'm Tallulah." The redhead waved like the Queen and continued arranging the scented potpourri.

Phew, thought Coral. At least she had officially been told their names now.

"This is for your hut," Coral said. "Welcome to Sunday Harbour. You'll notice it's heart-shaped."

Saffron accepted the lump of coral and looked at it carefully. "So it is. Thank you, it will look lovely with the pot plants on the deck."

Coral looked pleased and then nervous. "I thought you'd like it... seeing as you're all into romance and stuff." She smiled. Saffron smiled. Coral smiled some more. Saffron's smile started to droop at the corners. "Anyway, I just wanted to tell you about the Cupid Company," Coral added quickly, before she lost her audience.

"Do they make those lovely little summer frocks I've seen everyone wearing?" asked Tallulah.

"Actually it's the business thingy-ma-jig I was telling you about," answered Coral. "That thing we do – you see, we're a matchmaking company."

Coral wasted no time in telling the girls all about her and Nicks's Cupid Company head office at Coral Hut – the questionnaires, their past successes and the Cupid Company motto: All for love and love for all.

Neither of the girls interrupted or asked questions along the way. They simply stared at her with blinking eyes, until she was eventually done.

"Aw, isn't that cute!" cried Saffron, wrinkling

her nose at her friend. Tallulah made a wrinkled-nose face back and returned to the helmet of potpourri.

"Well, it's not so much cute as a really valuable service," replied Coral flatly. Glamorous big-city girls or not – she would still like to be taken seriously.

"I bet it is," cooed Saffron while she sprayed Headquarters with what smelled like lily-of-the-valley room freshener. The hut certainly smelled like lilies in a valley. The Captain would not be pleased. Saffron sighed and smiled. "There, that's better. This place was just too awful before."

"I always thought that this was a very useful sort of beach hut," said Coral. "I mean, you just never know when you might need a brass bugle."

Saffron thought about this and smiled gently, almost patronisingly. "So tell me more about this really valuable service you offer at the Cupid Company."

Coral took a deep breath and gulped. It was now or never. "How about we *show* you and help Sienna find love again?"

"SIENNA?" both girls echoed. The idea had obviously come from somewhere unexpected.

"I don't think…" mumbled Saffron.

"She's not ready…" burbled Tallulah.

Great, more people who think like Nicks… groaned the voice inside Coral's head. She would have to convince them, but there was no time now. Sienna had just returned with ice cream and Chanel. She still looked better than yesterday, but now her lipgloss had disappeared beneath ice cream and her face was dark with a scowl. She seemed very annoyed with the world.

"Stupid beach activities!" she growled, kicking at the crumbling ruins of a long-forgotten sandcastle in her path. Ice cream dripped down her arm and she licked at it ferociously, almost devouring her elbow at the same time. She then plopped down on a striped towel in front of Headquarters and focused entirely on her ice cream. A seagull overhead was the only thing to distract her.

"WOULD YOU BE QUIET!" she hollered at the cawing bird. "Or else I'm coming after ya!" The sweet and serene Sienna of yesterday was long gone. And so, it seemed, was that seagull.

"So who would you have in mind," whispered Saffron nervously, "you know – for Sienna... if we were to go ahead with your Cupid Company?"

Coral glanced at the very angry girl with the ice cream. She thought of Harry guiltily. But Sienna's fury was only temporary – she just needed to find love again, Coral reminded herself.

"Harry," she blurted out. "He runs the Beach Huts Association. And he's a very nice, non-cheating sort of guy. I'm quite sure he doesn't like football. Or football supporters for that matter either."

"Well, that's a good start," murmured

Saffron in a distracted sort of way. She was watching Sienna, who was now slapping irritably at an invisible sea breeze that was skipping through her hair. The sea breeze pranced past Saffron and then snagged on the questionnaire in Coral's fingers. The paper crackled as it danced with the breeze in her hands. Coral suddenly thought of Nicks. She would be annoyed if Coral didn't hand the questionnaire over.

So she held the shimmying paper out to Saffron. "Do you think you could fill this in on Sienna's behalf? It's Cupid Company policy." She shrugged apologetically. But Saffron was too busy watching Sienna, who was now glaring at a hermit crab burrowing alongside her. It looked like the questionnaire would be the least of Saffron's problems.

heart·stopping

As far as Coral could tell, the girls had left their beach hut some time ago. They'd clearly had no choice but to try and distract Sienna with some other activity.

Harry had come and gone too. He'd understood that his future date was not feeling well (it was only a lie of sorts) but this left Coral and Nicks and Romeo quite alone. Romeo was licking the salt off his paws, Nicks was writing in her diary and Coral was staring out to sea, bored and frustrated. She'd really imagined herself in her sunglasses and scarf with the sparkle stripe running through it, spending the afternoon with her neighbours.

Instead, she now stood slouched against the deck's railings, watching a large man and a boy with a watering can on the beach. The large man lay flat on his broad back on a straining sunlounger. The boy filled the can with cold seawater and tipped it over the man, who didn't flinch, not even a bit. The boy refilled the watering can and poured it over the man again. He made the trip backwards and forwards at least three times, and still the large man never even stirred. Perhaps it saved him the trouble of going for a swim?

Coral's bored gaze then settled on the red hut next door. They hadn't seen Scary Guy for a while, but she wasn't complaining. Still, as she looked closer, she could see some conspicuous stains on the deck steps. *Red* stains. They looked like red drips, to be precise. There were similar stains on the hut's deck too. They looked very much like drops of blood. *BLOOD?!*

"NIIIICCCCCCKS!"

Coral's friend reacted in an instant and jumped to her feet. "What! What is it?"

"COME AND LOOK! HERE!" Coral cried.

Nicks's eyes frantically scanned the region targeted by Coral's trembling pointed finger. She searched for any signs of madness and mayhem. Next she looked for some kind of mild disorder that might have caused her friend to panic. But everything appeared quite normal.

"What am I supposed to be looking at?" she enquired firmly.

"THERE!" yelled Coral like it was the most obvious thing ever. "The blood!"

Nicks squinted her eyes to focus. Finally, she noticed the drips of red. "You think that's blood?"

"What else could it be?"

"Tomato ketchup?"

Coral gave an *as if!* sort of grunt. "Scary Guy hardly looks like the takeaway type."

Nicks tapped her chin thoughtfully. "But blood?"

"I'm surprised you're even surprised," cried Coral. "The hammer, the rope and duct tape... It's hardly sugar, spice and all things nice, is it!"

Now Nicks looked pensive. "I guess not. So what should we do?"

"We need to tell someone," said Coral.

"Our parents?"

Coral thought about her mum and dad. They very rarely bought into her stories these days (so, she'd been wrong a few times before). "Nope," she replied. "We need to report Scary Guy to the Beach Patrol."

"The Beach Patrol? Mmm. Maybe we should wait and gather a bit more evidence first," suggested Nicks.

"It might be too late then! And dangerous,"

shrieked Coral. "No, we must act now. Come on, Nicks. Come on, Romeo."

The pup sat upright and blinked at the bright sunlight. He'd been dreaming of doggy choc drops. His legs bowed and he slumped to the floor again. The choc drops were calling him back to his dream.

"Come on, Romeo!" Coral cried again, already standing on the warm beach sand with her hands clenched. She was feeling bold and brave and grateful that she'd been blessed with hawk eyes. Thanks to her the beach hut community would soon be safe again. And what a story that would make!

Nicks and Romeo finally followed, never quite managing to keep up with Coral, who was taking great strides and swinging her arms determinedly. They crossed the beach (making sure to side-step sand sculptures, small children, horizontal bodies and one snoozing head sticking out of the sand). They zigzagged in between the white hulls of beached sailing boats and hobbled with their bare feet over the cobbled jetty. Up ahead, the lifeguards' station was a neat, rough-brick building with very large square windows and various flags sticking out of its flat roof. And in a smaller side-building with its own entrance was the office of Sunday Harbour's Beach Patrol. If anybody missed the sign saying as much, they couldn't miss the silver metal bicycle rack alongside it. Most of the Beach Patrol officers went around on bicycles.

Coral held the door open for Nicks and Romeo, feeling very much in charge. And then she led them to the first desk closest to the door where a girl with sunstreaked hair was chewing gum and scribbling on a pad. Coral coughed.

Finally the girl looked up at them with her very green eyes. "Uh huh?"

"We have a possible crime scene to report," said Coral importantly, while Nicks chewed on her lip and felt just a teensy bit silly (a possible crime scene… possible tomato ketchup… who could say… except Coral, obviously).

Coral expected the girl with the green eyes to leap to her feet and immediately bark loud orders across the room. She expected cries of alarm and an energised posse of Beach Patrol bicycles to gather outside in less than two minutes flat. Instead, the girl silently chewed her gum and stared up at Coral.

"Littering?" she finally asked while she chewed.

Was the girl asking if the crime they were reporting was littering? Coral didn't even know that littering was a crime (not that she was a litterbug). She shook her head hotly.

The green eyes blinked twice. "Graffiti? Double-parking? Petty larceny?"

Now Coral blinked. "Pardon?"

The green eyes blinked. "Larceny… means theft."

"Oh, right. No. I don't think anybody stole anything."

Finally the girl did something. "Ramone!" she called out.

A very tanned man about four desks back stood up slowly. When he'd finally reached his full height (he was very tall) he lifted his square jaw and surveyed the room quietly with his black, heavy eyes. His hair was thick, dark and soft, and rippled like small waves as he flicked his head to move a curl that was obscuring his smouldering gaze. He then stuck his thumbs in the waist of his denim shorts and ambled in a leisurely manner over to where they stood. The girls watched him, mesmerised. *He would definitely make the perfect romantic lead in a film*, thought Coral.

Now that he was closer they could smell his musky aftershave. Romeo sneezed and Nicks's nose twitched, but Coral liked the smell. It reminded her of the scented furniture polish her grandmother used. His tanned skin was almost as brown as her grandmother's furniture too, so it was a good-memories sort of smell.

"What can I do for you girls?" he finally said in a voice that was so deep it took a few moments for his words to settle and make sense.

"We have a crime to report," revealed Coral, confident with the scent of her grandmother's furniture polish in her nostrils.

"We think... a uh, *possible* crime," added Nicks nervously.

"Let's take a seat over there then," suggested Ramone as he flicked his dark curls in the direction of a small round table and chairs to the side of the room. The girls sat down, but Ramone perched on the edge of the table with one foot dangling. "Now tell me about this crime," he ordered gently.

Coral didn't need to be told twice. "There's blood splattered across the deck of our neighbour's beach hut!"

"She thinks... er, *we think* it might be blood," added Nicks quickly (but not before taking a very deep breath, which was what

103

being best friends sometimes required).

"What makes you think it might be blood?" asked Ramone, as patiently and calmly as if they'd just told him it was sunny outside.

Coral tried not to let her disappointment show; she felt sure he'd panic just as soon as he heard their entire story. So she immediately launched into a vivid description of Scary Guy and his bag of torture instruments and the shadows and the strange noises that had come from his beach hut. She was almost out of breath from the effort by the time she was done.

But still Ramone did not panic. Instead, he sat there, swinging his leg to and fro, staring between his curls at Coral. And then finally he spoke.

"What colour did you say the hut was?"

Finally! He was obviously preparing to head over immediately.

"It's glossy and red!" cried Coral with relief.

"And the drops on the deck are red too, hmm?"

"Well, yes, but…" stammered Coral. "What's that got to do with anything?"

"There's the Best Beach Hut competition coming up. Maybe your neighbour is just doing a bit of DIY in preparation?"

"But we've never seen him do any painting," replied Coral seriously.

"But you're not at your hut all the time, are you?" said Ramone.

"Of course not, but I think we'd notice if he'd painted his hut." Coral looked to Nicks for confirmation, but her best friend suddenly seemed unsure. Her face said that Ramone might have a point.

"But what about the stuff in his bag?" pleaded Coral.

"A hammer, duct tape… it all sounds like standard DIY tools." Ramone shrugged like he was almost sorry.

"But what about Scary Guy?!" Coral finally cried out. "He's seriously scary!"

Nicks blushed a rosy pink. They'd been told

many times never to judge someone by their appearance. She suddenly felt rather guilty. "Maybe we should just get going," she mumbled. "And we'll uh, get in touch if anything else happens."

Coral turned to Nicks and stared, outraged. "Ramone should at the very least take forensic samples of the red drops!"

"*Coral*," Nicks hissed through clenched teeth. She was still a very pink colour.

"That hut is private property. We'd need a much better reason than the ones you've given me to take forensic samples." The corners of Ramone's mouth curled when he spoke the last two words. "And besides, that would be a job for the police. But I will make you girls a promise. I will keep an eye on the red hut for you. And if anything happens, you can be sure we'll be on the case immediately."

Coral thought about this for a moment. It wasn't the wild panic or screams of alarm or the posse of Beach Patrol bicycles she'd imagined, but it would have to do. For the moment. She was never wrong. Well, hardly ever. OK, maybe sometimes. But not often. She left the Beach Patrol office feeling sure that she wasn't wrong *this time...*

heartburn

They arrived back at the beach hut with Romeo in tow. Coral was the first one to notice Saffron sitting on the deck of Headquarters. She waved and received a wave in return. The whole *I'm-so-happy-I-could-scream* thing Coral had going on with her neighbours seemed to have run its course, and for this she was very happy (but not in a screaming sort of way).

"I have that questionnaire for you," the older girl called out.

Romeo was already halfway up the minty-green, pink and lemon deck steps, but Coral went the way of the khaki painted steps instead to where Saffron was untangling a cut-glass suncatcher. "That is pretty," she said.

"I'm going to hang it from the roof." Saffron demonstrated by dangling the now tangle-free suncatcher in the air. "I have lots more just like it." She seemed very pleased about it too. And Coral had to admit that Headquarters did look very different these days. It looked less army and a lot more glittery. It was colourful and shiny, just like its new occupants. In fact there were very few signs of Birdie and the Captain left. The army cot was now covered in a cream and gold quilt of stitched satin and scattered sequins. The rest of the hut was decorated with delicate tealight lamps, pink glass perfume bottles, scarves, feathers and flowers.

Coral's eyeball tour ended at Saffron, who

was now holding out a completed questionnaire. Coral accepted the paper, but didn't give it a glance. She'd wait for Nicks to do that. And besides, she had more important things to worry about – like Scary Guy. Nobody was safe while the case of the blood on the deck went unsolved.

"The other girls will be back soon," said Saffron.

"I hope Sienna is feeling better," replied Coral awkwardly. This was her chance – her opportunity to spend some quality time with one of her fabulous new neighbours, but she just couldn't think past Scary Guy.

Saffron shrugged. "Not really. But she will. I hope. Eventually." She sighed deeply, like just the mention of the subject exhausted her.

Coral still really wanted to help – she wanted to help all the girls. And finding Sienna a new love might just have been the one-stop solution to the problem. "Non-cheating Harry, who runs the Beach Huts Association, said he would stop by today," she remembered out loud. "Shall we introduce him to Sienna?"

Saffron chewed her glossy bottom lip and nodded. "I guess we could do." She shrugged like it certainly couldn't make things any worse.

Suddenly there was a *bang*. Coral jumped like a gun had gone off in her ear. She twisted in the direction of the sound. But it was just Nicks opening up the double doors of Coral Hut.

"Thanks for the questionnaire," Coral said finally, with a diluted sort of smile. "And I'm sure Harry is the one."

"That would be nice," replied Sienna hopefully.

Coral left with her eyes down, scanning the sandy surrounds for any more possible drips of blood. She reached the top of Coral Hut's steps and stared long and hard at the red hut. She needed something she could take back to Ramone. She waited and listened and watched carefully. But the red hut was fast asleep.

Nicks was not quite as patient, and quickly tugged the questionnaire from Coral's grip. "Mmm," she said as she read. "So Sienna likes make-up, the colour purple, salon music, MySpace, vanilla coffee, compact mirrors and collecting belts and socks. She dislikes flying bugs and…"

But Coral wasn't listening. She was thinking about some form of alarm system that would let her know when Scary Guy arrived (or left) the red hut. Ramone had said that she should keep tabs on him. Sort of.

A piece of string with a bell attached to it might do it. She could stretch it across the bottom of the red beach hut's steps (in which case, better make it transparent fishing gut instead of string). She would no doubt find a bell in the box of Christmas decorations in the loft at home. The plan in her head was coming together nicely.

Nicks was still reading from the questionnaire.

"Sienna's hobbies are looking at wedding dresses and nail art. Mmm. You know, I'm not so sure that Sienna is right for Harry." She glanced up from the questionnaire. Her best friend was pressed up flat against the front of Coral Hut and peering at the red hut next door.

"What are you doing?"

"Nothing really – just testing out a few angles."

Nicks refused to even ask. "So anyway, it's like I was saying, Harry is all about saving the world and Sienna is all about saving a nail."

Coral tried to look interested, but her gaze kept slipping over to the hut next door. Scary Guy moved quickly; until she had that alarm installed she could not allow herself to be distracted.

"I know that opposites attract, but this time I really don't think that Harry and Sienna are well suited," concluded Nicks firmly.

"Harry!" cried Coral.

Nicks turned to find their newest Cupid Company client standing there wearing a SAVE OUR SEA LIONS T-shirt.

"Hi, girls." He smiled bashfully and pushed his glasses further up his nose. Today his hair was extra stand-up-spiky and he looked quite handsome. It was a good day for him to meet Sienna, thought Coral.

"I'm sorry, Harry," said Nicks, "but it looks as if the Cupid Company still needs a few more days to find you the right girl."

Harry's smile slipped down at the corners.

"Of course we don't!" cried Coral. "In fact, she'll be here any minute."

Harry's smile curled up once again.

Nicks coughed. "No, no, we really need a little more time…"

Coral slapped the air. "Time slime. This girl is very sophisticated."

Harry's eyes grew wider.

"Er, maybe a bit too sophisticated," hissed Nicks through her teeth.

Harry seemed to slump.

Coral kept her eyes and smile firm and in place. "But Nicks, that's like saying *too much chocolate*." Her face had a look of impossibility to it.

"Exactly!" growled Nicks. Too much of anything could never be good, she firmly believed.

Harry now officially had no idea what they were talking about. His face seemed to give up and fall flat. And then the rest of the girls arrived next door at Headquarters, including Sienna. This might be a good day to present Harry to Sienna, but would it be a good day to present Sienna to Harry? Coral felt nervous. She craned her head to get a better view of the recently dumped girl and was pleased to discover that she was mascara-streak free. Her hair was brushed and swept back in a jewelled clip. And her clothes were neat and showed no signs of leftover comfort foods. But she still looked a little annoyed with the world.

Harry's eyes followed Coral's gaze. "Is that her?" he asked.

"Yes," whispered Coral conspiratorially. She watched the girls very closely; it was important that they chose their moment carefully.

Harry smiled. "She is pretty!"

Pretty Sienna kicked angrily at a stray beach ball in her path. It flew for metres and narrowly missed a man carrying two tall orange drinks.

Coral chuckled nervously while her mind worked overtime. Arranging a one-on-one first date would not be a good idea. A casual, group introduction was definitely the better (and safer) option, for Harry especially.

Nicks had obviously still not come around to Coral's way of thinking and her face was silent and frowning. But Harry clearly couldn't wait another moment.

"Come on!" he called out merrily as he made his way over to the hut next door. So Coral grabbed Nicks's hand and pulled her along with an encouraging friendly smile. After all, there was no Cupid Company without Nicks.

They found Saffron, Tallulah and Chanel swapping make-up while Sienna sat in a corner, using black eyeliner to draw a curly moustache on the cover girl of a magazine. The brokenhearted girl still looked surly. Saffron was the first to glance up. Coral flicked her eyes and made small jerky head movements in Harry's direction. The older girl seemed to understand.

"Oh, look, we have visitors!" she said in a very jolly voice. The other girls also seemed to know what to expect because they stood up and made a point of looking bright and breezy. Only Sienna sat slumped in her corner. She was now very busily blacking out one of the cover girl's white front teeth.

Coral waved hello and then pointed like a tour guide to Harry. "This is our friend Harry," she revealed.

Harry grinned and looked very pleased.

"Hi, Harry," they all said, except for Sienna, who had decided to black out the rest of the cover girl's teeth too. And then finally she glanced up. Harry seemed more pleased than ever. Sienna looked from Harry's grin to his SAVE OUR SEA LIONS T-shirt. And then she suddenly and unexpectedly burst into a torrent of tears. She threw her head back and wailed while water spewed from her eyes like a leaking fire extinguisher.

The jolly smiles were instantly replaced by confused, concerned faces. *Where had it all gone wrong?*

"What's the matter?" stammered Tallulah.

But Sienna was crying so desperately she couldn't speak for a few moments. She howled and blubbed and then finally managed to gasp, "HIS T-SHIRT!"

There was only one boy there that day, and every head – including Harry's – suddenly snapped in the direction of his T-shirt. It still said SAVE OUR SEA LIONS. They all looked more confused than ever.

Sienna breathed deep to control her sobs,

hiccupped loudly and finally cried out, "That was my nickname for Sam!"

Sam was the cheating ex-boyfriend. BUT *SAVE OUR SEA LIONS*? It was a very strange nickname indeed.

The general confusion was not lost on Sienna, whose misery was now tinged with irritation. "SEA LION!" she roared and then wailed some more. "Sammy," she spluttered, "the sea lion... I used to call him my little sea lion!"

Now they all got it – well, everyone except for Harry. He had no idea why this girl would be so upset by Sammy the sea lion.

Saffron patted her friend's heaving shoulder, Chanel rushed for a box of tissues and Tallulah shook her head miserably as if to say, *One SAVE OUR SEA LIONS T-shirt and we're back to square one.* It looked like her dreamy seaside holiday was becoming more of a seaside nightmare. And then Scary Guy sauntered past carrying a life-sized skeleton and a shovel!

bravehearts

Coral's mouth and eyes flew wide open. She was used to seeing skeletons – she regularly stared unfocused at the skeleton in their biology class at school (it was not her strongest subject). But seeing one clatter past the row of beach huts – being carried by Scary Guy – was something entirely different. *And what about that shovel!*

Nobody else really seemed to take any notice

of it, and it was only when Coral started spluttering and pointing that Nicks paid any attention. Except by then it was too late. Scary Guy had already disappeared inside his hut.

"What is wrong with you?" hissed Nicks.

Finally Coral let out a small, high-pitched scream while Sienna continued to wail. It combined to create quite a chaotic scene.

Saffron leaned over and whispered hoarsely at the two younger girls. "I really don't think that this is the right time for the *I'm so-happy-I-could scream* thing!"

But Coral barely even heard her. "I saw Scary Guy carrying a skeleton and a shovel!"

Nicks's head spun this way and that. "What? Where? When?"

"Right now! But he's disappeared inside his hut already!"

Nicks frowned while she gave this some thought. Her friend was known for her runaway imagination. But then Scary Guy suddenly emerged from the hut, only this time his hands were empty. The girls watched, mesmerised, while the tall, very thin man disappeared down the beach, striding purposefully and muttering to himself. He hadn't noticed them at all and seemed preoccupied. In fact he was so preoccupied he'd forgotten to close the hut's double doors properly. The girls stared at the pole of bright sunlight that suddenly fell through the gap in the doors and landed inside the red hut.

It was now or never, thought Coral.

Nicks sighed. "Maybe we should just forget about Scary Guy for the moment."

Sienna, meanwhile, had been ushered inside Headquarters and was now resting on the cream and gold quilt of stitched satin and scattered sequins that covered the Captain's army cot. She had stopped sobbing, and only wailed every now and again, when she remembered. Everyone looked quite relieved (except for Coral, of course). She was twitching and feeling quite close to internally combusting.

"Your hut really is quite lovely," commented Harry, who still had no real idea what had just happened, but clearly found these four new girls very pretty nonetheless. He reached inside his pocket and pulled out a Best Beach Hut competition leaflet. "It would be a shame if you didn't enter," he said, handing it over. "And I should know – I work for the Beach Huts Association." He nodded and rocked on his heels importantly.

The older girls huddled over the leaflet while Coral leaned into Nicks.

"Come on – we have to take a peek inside Scary Guy's hut."

"WHAAT?!" cried Nicks.

"Ramone said that we should keep a close eye on him! And this may be the only chance we get to see what's really going on inside the hut next door."

"It's breaking and entering, Coral."

"Not if the door is open it's not."

"Well, OK, but it's still trespassing."

"The man has a skeleton inside his hut!" snapped Coral. "And what about the blood. And the duct tape. And all that other scary stuff."

"That could all prove to be nothing."

"Then Scary Guy has nothing to hide," reasoned Coral. "But we must be sure that there's nothing sinister going on. Then we can report back to Ramone."

Nicks seemed to consider this. *Poking around the red hut might just put an end to Coral's accusations.* Nicks had to admit that even she found Scary Guy slightly suspicious. Perhaps this really was the best way to stop the craziness once and for all. "Oh, all right then," she finally agreed.

Sienna was still lolling indoors, but the other three girls seemed very interested in hearing about the Best Beach Hut competition. They didn't even notice Coral and Nicks disappear.

The two girls approached the red hut cautiously. They were wary of Scary Guy returning and catching them nosing about, but he was nowhere to be seen. Close up, the hut looked as bright, but a little less shiny. There were worn, dull patches on the steps where feet had traipsed up and down over time, but the rest of the exterior of the hut was quite plain.

The red double doors opened wider with a faint squeaking sound. Inside, the hut looked quite sombre after the glaring sunshine outside, and it took a few moments for shapes to emerge from the hut's shadows. The girls waited nervously. In a corner to the right a desk with a chair appeared. The top of the desk was mostly hidden beneath sheets of paper covered in scrawl. There were also two plastic cups crammed with pencil stubs and... *A KNIFE!*

Actually, it was more of a penknife, but that was still a knife, and a potential weapon (and murdering instrument). Both girls' eyes stretched wider. A large chalkboard on legs emerged from a wall opposite the desk. The girls took a few steps closer. White words appeared on the chalkboard: SUFFOCATE. STRANGLE. THROW BODY OVERBOARD. POISON.

The warm air inside the hut caught at the back of the girls' throats and made a wheezing sound as they gasped. There were also yellow Post-its stuck all around the chalkboard's wooden frame. And each Post-it contained a single phrase scratched in looping, crazed handwriting: BOTTOM OF RIVER. BUNGLED BURGLARY. MISSING PERSON. FIRE POKER WITH FINGERPRINTS. GLOVES FORGOTTEN AT CRIME SCENE.

This was more than Coral had ever imagined. She teetered backwards and collided with the skeleton lounging in an old stuffed armchair, which was the only other piece of furniture inside the hut. There was no time left to hesitate.

"Come on, let's get out of here!" cried Nicks hoarsely.

Coral only needed to be told once and, in a matter of moments, they'd leaped from the fading, trodden red steps and had landed in the soft, hot beach sand. They kept on going and only stopped when they were once again safe and sound inside the beautiful and very beachy Coral Hut. Their little shrine to love felt like a world away from the terrifying hut next door, but still it took the girls a few moments to find their breath. And at least they now had their beloved pup Romeo for protection.

taken to heart

"We must tell Ramone immediately!" gasped Coral. She patted her leg to hurry Romeo along, but he didn't seem particularly concerned as he lay sprawled beneath the daybed with a small red chew-ball between his paws.

"So do we really think Scary Guy is a criminal?" said Nicks, almost pleadingly.

"He's quite obviously nutty. And that hut..." huffed Coral, "... is clearly where he plans the carnage! Now come on, we must get over to Beach Patrol quickly. Romeo!"

The pup's snubby snout appeared from beneath the daybed, the red chew-ball still in his mouth. He hesitated.

Coral hopped from one foot to the other. "Oh all right, bring the ball then! Now come on, you two."

And off they went, stepping double-time across the beach and over the cobbled jetty towards the rough-brick building they had only just visited. But the girl with the green eyes was missing. In her place was a different girl with a square face, a long nose and dark freckles that matched her hair. She had soft, chubby cheeks and kind, gentle eyes.

"Hello, can I help you?" she said politely.

"We have to see Ramone!" bleated Coral.

"He's just stepped out for a moment," replied the girl. "Is everything all right?"

Coral didn't need to be asked twice. Everything was *not* all right – not even close, and she was very eager to tell somebody about it. And if Ramone wasn't around, then this girl would have to do. So she let fly with her story about Scary Guy and the red hut and the blood drips and murderous words and (pen) knife and concluded with a mention of the skeleton that had practically attacked her.

The girl sat there silently, her small eyes stretched as big and round as the moon. "Wow," she exclaimed when Coral was finally done.

"Exactly! Now you know why we have to speak to Ramone."

The girl nodded seriously and stared at Coral like she was very brave to have endured that sort of situation. This wasn't lost on Coral, who puffed out her chest and set her jaw in a solemn sort of way. She was feeling rather courageous. Nicks, on the other hand, just looked really anxious. She still couldn't believe that their beach hut neighbour might be a madman. Nothing very exciting (or dangerous) usually happened in Sunday Harbour and it was all rather difficult to comprehend.

"Do you want a drink of water while you wait?" asked the girl.

Coral considered the offer and shook her head. She was too caught up in the drama of the moment. Nicks looked too nervous to drink anything. And Romeo had already helped himself to the drops of water dripping from the nearby water cooler. He stood there with his red chew-ball between his paws and his tongue out while Coral paced up and down and Nicks bit on her knuckle.

"My name is Grace," said the girl.

"Have you worked here long?" asked Nicks, who thought that small talk might take their minds off the bigger (vaguely terrifying) picture.

"Actually I'm a volunteer," replied Grace. "I work as often as they need me, which is quite often." She chuckled, spied Coral's stern face and quickly stopped again. And then Ramone appeared, strutting boldly down the corridor with his long brown legs and swaying shoulders setting the pace.

"So you're back," he said when he saw the girls.

"And they have something very important to tell you," Grace revealed supportively.

Ramone smiled a half-smile that was almost a smirk. "Oh, do they now?"

Coral ignored this and quickly and clearly repeated what she had just told Grace, the very nice volunteer. And Ramone listened, although he didn't seem as impressed at the end.

"Your neighbour's door may have been open, but that's still trespassing," he finally said.

Coral stared. Was he being serious? Ramone returned her stare. It seemed so.

"But he's a crazy, scary guy!" cried Coral.

Other people in the Beach Patrol office quickly looked up.

Ramone's hands pressed down on the air like he was taming a whirlwind. "Now calm down. I will come and take a proper look, OK?"

Both Coral and Nicks sighed with relief.

"Can I come along too?" asked Grace suddenly. She jumped up and attempted to escape from behind the desk, but the lace of her trainer had become hooked in the leg of her chair and she was stuck fast.

Ramone made an 'erm' sound while Grace pulled frantically at her leg.

"Oh, PLEASE! How will I ever get any training sitting behind this desk?" said Grace. "And you did say I was ready to go on patrol."

Ramone still seemed unsure.

"You know all I've ever wanted to do is serve the community," added Grace, whose face had changed from sweet to stubborn. "And I'm not getting any experience sitting behind this desk." She then used her free leg to kick the desk like it was to blame. Ramone, Coral and Nicks all flinched at once. Nice-girl Grace's flash of temper had surprised them all.

"Fine, you can be my partner," agreed Ramone. The Beach Patrol usually went out in pairs – even in a peaceful place like Sunday Harbour. And then he turned to Coral and Nicks. "We'll be along soon enough. I just need to make a written report first."

Make a written report, echoed the voice inside Coral's head importantly. *Now that's more like it!* Finally they were being taken seriously.

"You're probably better off referring to me as 'Coral of Coral Hut'," said Coral of Coral Hut, "you know – just to make your report crystal clear."

Nicks rolled her eyes, Ramone stared at his reflection in the polished window opposite and Grace hurriedly scribbled the words 'Coral of Coral Hut' on her official Beach Patrol notepad. Released from deskwork (but not yet her desk), she was already on the case.

heart·throb

Coral and Nicks sat on the deck of their beach hut, waiting to see a pair of Beach Patrol bicycles, while Romeo played with a new furry friend he'd found. The dog was a collie and more than twice his size, but still Romeo took the role of pursuer. The two dogs raced in circles with their tongues dangling and grins that stretched as far back as their flying ears. They were as cheery as Coral and Nicks were not.

The best friends sat silent and watchful. Nicks leaned against her deck chair and watched the dogs while Coral's head moved this way and that way and back again. It looked like she was watching a game of tennis, but really she was just alternating between a view of the red hut *(so where was Scary Guy?)* and the promenade *(so where were Ramone and Grace?)*. She was so preoccupied that she'd even forgotten about her mission to get to know the older girls next door better.

Harry had disappeared, but the girls were suntanning on the sand in front of Headquarters. They were reading romance novels, dressed in flowery bikinis and sequined sarongs and looked pretty, painted and perfumed. Not that Coral really noticed. She barely even glanced in their direction. Not even her beloved pup could distract her; the case of Scary Guy occupied all her thoughts.

Finally Ramone and Grace came cycling along the promenade wearing helmets and riding on big, shiny silver Beach Patrol bicycles. They pulled up at Coral Hut and stood their bikes on stands off the path. Grace's bike fell over twice, but eventually the pair cut a path between the beach huts and climbed the steps to the deck of the minty-green, pale pink and lemon-yellow hut.

"Oh, this is so pretty," commented Grace as she scribbled in her notebook.

But Ramone seemed uninterested in Coral Hut. He unclipped his helmet, put his chin to his chest and shook his head of thick, dark curls to remove any traces of hat hair. Finally he looked up. He turned to the red hut and gave it a mindful stare. Then he noticed the dogs playing on the beach. And then he looked down at the four girls suntanning in front of Headquarters. His eyes rested there the longest.

"So what do you think?" wondered an anxious Coral.

Ramone nodded with a quiet confidence.

"It's very interesting indeed…" He gazed out a bit longer and then turned back to the girls standing on the deck of Coral Hut. They stared back at him expectantly. "Perhaps we should do a perimeter inspection first," he finally suggested.

"Shall we create one of those barriers with yellow tape?" asked Coral, who had seen quite a few detective shows on television and knew all about preserving evidence. Nicks nodded; she'd seen all the same shows.

"A perimeter inspection means we're going to inspect the wider area," explained Grace as she scribbled in her notebook.

So they all followed Ramone's lead down the stairs. But instead of making a perimeter search in the direction of the red hut, he veered right and swaggered over to Headquarters with his shoulders back and his thumbs once again hooked in the belt of his denim shorts. He paused close to the khaki hut and straightened his spine before raising his square jaw to the sunlight.

"Now, I don't want you girls to worry yourselves," he said, louder than was really necessary. "Remember, I am here to protect you."

Coral and Nicks nodded and Grace made further notes in her book. Ramone swivelled his head left then right and resumed his original position with his tummy in and his chest out. "Now, from my initial inspection," he continued seriously, "everything seems to be in order. I can't see anything suspicious."

Coral frowned. He wasn't even inspecting the right hut. But Ramone had attracted the attention of the four girls lying on the sand in front of Headquarters. Like well-rehearsed dancers, they all rose up on their elbows and directed their sunglasses this way and that before finally resting their collective gaze on the tall, muscled man in front of them. Each girl sat up straight, breathed in, lowered her sunglasses and observed him closely.

None of this was lost on Ramone, who arched his back and puffed his chest out even more.

Then Tallulah flicked her hair playfully.

Saffron plumped up her glossy lips.

Chanel batted her eyelashes.

And Sienna stared with mild interest.

But Coral was the first to make a sound, and it was an irritated 'pssht' sort of noise. She turned in desperation to Grace, who seemed like her last hope. "Don't you think you should be taking a closer look at the *red hut*?"

Grace looked confused and slightly nervous. This was her first beach patrol and Ramone was the team leader, but she was inclined to agree with Coral.

"Er, Ramone?" she stammered.

"Mmm?" he murmured as he brought one foot forward and flexed a calf muscle.

"What about the red hut?"

He pressed his hand to his waist and tightened a bronzed bicep muscle. "Yes, good idea, Grace," he replied in a very deep voice. "You run along and take a closer look at the red hut. It'll be good practice for you while I interview the public." And by public he obviously meant the four pretty girls suntanning in front of the khaki hut because that was exactly where he headed.

Coral and Nicks watched him while Grace scribbled something in her notebook. She then looked up, grinned, and sighed happily. "Isn't this exciting! All I've ever wanted to do is work for the community! Now come on, let's go and take a look at the red hut. But remember, it is private property after all and *ndhhiw uighfgebd dkhkle...*"

Her words became a jumble; Coral's mind was elsewhere. The Beach Patrol had seemed like the answer to their problems, but now she wasn't so sure. It looked like they might just need a Plan B after all. Still, she followed Grace and waited patiently with Nicks while the newest member of Sunday Harbour's Beach

Patrol nattered and sketched the layout of the beach huts in her notebook.

Ramone was still interviewing the girls at Headquarters (while sharing Tallulah's towel) by the time Grace had finished, so she went on to take witness statements from Coral and Nicks. And then finally Ramone stood up, flexed one final time and slowly swaggered back in the direction of Coral Hut, where he paused and struck a pose.

"We must be vigilant!" he declared loudly. "We must increase our patrols of the area. We shall stop by at least three times a day."

Three times a day? Coral should have been pleased, but her instincts told her that these extra patrols would have very little to do with the red hut, or Scary Guy, for that matter.

heartfelt

From then on things seemed to go from bad to worse, or so Coral thought. But one good thing happened too: Nicks finally came around to her way of thinking. Of course Nicks had always had her suspicions about Scary Guy, but there had also been some leftover space in her mind for doubt. She'd never been as convinced that Scary Guy was up to no good. But the following morning changed all that. The two girls were sitting perched on the deck of Coral Hut, contemplating Harry's love life (or lack thereof, thanks to the Cupid Company) when Scary Guy appeared next door. Actually, he didn't appear so much as grow larger in the distance, until finally he walked right past Coral Hut and up the deck steps to his own beach hut. And he didn't walk so much as stagger (he was balancing a very large pile of books in his arms).

Coral and Nicks stopped breathing and sat silent with bug-eyes. Only their chins moved as they followed the man with the pulsing Adam's apple. He was still a scary guy. He looked taller and thinner than ever and was wearing a shirt with short sleeves that showed the fine network of blue throbbing veins beneath his white skin.

They watched as he freed up one arm and struggled to slip a key into the lock of the beach hut door. He'd just unlocked it when the book at the very top of the pile teetered, slipped and fell in slow motion. Coral and Nicks watched as Scary Guy tried to catch it. He reached out a bony hand; the knuckle of his long thin thumb was wrapped up in a bandage. The pile in his arms swayed dangerously. He quickly pulled his arm back again and steadied the tower – obviously deciding to sacrifice one book for the sake of the rest. The book landed on the floor, bounced, skidded across the decking and toppled down to the beach sand below. Scary Guy grunted. And then he disappeared behind the double red doors and did not come out again.

Both girls waited a few minutes to be sure. And then Coral stuck her head over the edge of the deck of Coral Hut. She stared down at Scary Guy's book, resisting the urge for as many moments as she could, and then she disappeared in a blur down the deck steps before reappearing with the book.

"You can't take it!" hissed Nicks.

But Coral didn't reply. She was too busy

studying the book's cover. Finally she held it upright for Nicks to see. *FAMOUS COPYCAT MURDERS*, it read.

It was as if time had stopped. The world went quiet as the girls stared at each other and blinked nervously. There was no doubting Scary Guy now.

"What do you think is going on with his bandaged thumb?" whispered Coral in a deep, sinister tone.

Nicks bit her lip and stared at her best friend.

"He probably cut himself – you know... *MURDERING!*" muttered Coral menacingly.

Nicks nodded, like of course she'd thought the same all along.

"We're going to have to come up with a Plan B," added Coral.

Nicks nodded and then looked confused. "What was Plan A?"

Coral sighed. "Plan A was Ramone and the Beach Patrol. But he obviously doesn't take this case seriously, so we need a Plan B. We need to conduct our own surveillance. And we need more evidence. We'll use your camera to take photos of everything we find, including Scary Guy."

Nicks nodded again and then both girls sat in thoughtful silence for a few moments. Neither could forget that Scary Guy *(a copycat murderer?)* was right next door – just a few metres away. So they were specially pleased when their other neighbours arrived at Headquarters.

Nicks and Coral waved vigorously. The older girls waved back. They seemed just as delighted to see their younger neighbours.

Saffron looked more sparkly than ever and Tallulah, who had curled her long red hair, waved a set of nails she'd specially painted with silver and pink hearts. "Yoo-hoo girls!" she called out.

Coral and Nicks waved once more.

"So has the Beach Patrol been past yet?" Chanel called out while her friends waited with round eyes and big glossy O-lips. Even Sienna looked perky.

Coral shrugged. She certainly hadn't seen the Beach Patrol and there didn't seem to be much point in encouraging the visits either, especially not now that their neighbours had secured Ramone's interest. Her shoulders slumped. Things were not going as planned. The Beach Patrol did not seem particularly interested in solving the mystery of Scary Guy (Mr Copycat Murderer who was right next door at that very moment!). And Sienna did not seem vaguely interested in Harry. And Scary Guy was quite a lot to worry about, so it would have been nice if for once love could have done as it was told. Poor Harry!

And then, as if on cue, Harry came striding along the beach, carrying what looked like a wad of orange plastic sheets, before stopping in front of the beach huts.

"Hello, girls," he said as he glanced from the older girls to Coral and Nicks. Everyone waved half-heartedly. They were all obviously preoccupied with thoughts of either Ramone or Scary Guy. But Harry didn't seem to mind. He just seemed happy to be there.

"It's Anti-Litter Week!" he announced grandly, flapping the orange sheets in the air. He then peeled one from the wad and found its opening. The orange sheet was in fact a plastic rubbish bag printed with the slogan, KEEP SUNDAY HARBOUR CLEAN. "Would you like one?" Harry asked.

"Definitely," replied Nicks. She'd never liked litter either.

The older girls all looked at one another with baffled expressions. They'd clearly never met a conscientious lad like Harry before. It was Saffron who leaned over the deck railings for a bag.

Harry beamed. "Here you go, girls! And do you know that the most common type of litter is cigarette ends, followed closely by sweet and crisp packets?"

Nobody spoke, but there was a lot of blank staring and blinking. Harry was not put off. The subject was of particular interest to him.

"The Alliance is considering introducing on-the-spot fines for littering," he proudly announced. "I'm a member of the Alliance, you know." The sea breeze sounded louder than ever. "It's actually called the Community Alliance. We work with the council to make sure that Sunday Harbour remains the lovely seaside town it is today." He gestured broadly with his hands as he admired his surroundings.

Saffron, Sienna, Chanel and Tallulah tracked his hands with their heads. They stopped when Harry stopped, and then they stared some more. They looked bored. Sienna especially looked restless. She turned and scanned the horizon. Harry was too busy talking about litter to really notice that she was looking out for somebody else. But Coral wasn't.

She let Harry continue and waited with words on her tongue, ready to jump the moment he paused. "That really is fascinating, Harry!" she cheered and clapped the first chance she got.

The older girls glanced over at Coral Hut. They were looking baffled again. Was Coral being funny? Even Harry looked surprised, like his litter speech wasn't usually applauded.

Coral pushed on regardless. "I think it is great what you do for Sunday Harbour – you know, working with the Community Alliance *and* the Beach Huts Association. You're one great guy!"

Harry shrugged bashfully, like it was nothing.

"And honest," added Coral.

Harry grinned and rocked on his heels. "Well, I believe it is the best policy."

"And that means you're definitely a non-cheater." Now Coral sneaked a look at Sienna. The heartbroken girl seemed to consider this for a brief moment. She even appeared slightly curious. And then the look disappeared again and she was left looking bored and gazing out at the horizon once more. Coral sagged, like all her enthusiasm had suddenly left her. Maybe Nicks was right; perhaps Sienna wasn't the one for Harry after all. But the afternoon hadn't been a complete waste of time – at least they'd forgotten about Scary Guy for a short while.

SCARY GUY!

Coral stood ramrod straight. Was he still locked up in the hut next door (possibly planning his next copycat murder)?

16

wild at heart

"Do you think I could have a quiet word?" whispered Harry hoarsely. "You know... alone?"

"Er..." mumbled Coral. Her gaze was still fixed on the red hut next door, so Nicks discreetly gestured Harry over to Coral Hut's deck (although the girls at Headquarters seemed to have lost interest anyway).

Harry looked uncomfortable. "I don't want to seem ungrateful," he stammered, "but I'm

53

just not convinced that Sienna is the girl for me."

Finally Coral's head turned away from the hut. "Yes, we know," she agreed with a firm nod, "and we're on the case."

"*You are?*" said Harry.

"*We are?*" said Nicks at exactly the same time. But Coral was already focused on the red hut once more.

Nicks smiled at Harry kindly. "Yes, we'll have the perfect date for you very soon!"

"You will?"

"Definitely. Come back tomorrow, OK?"

Harry nodded and disappeared with his bright orange bags flapping in the breeze. Nicks watched him thoughtfully while Coral reached for her best friend's camera. She peered through the lens at the red hut, then removed the cap, and peered once more. And then something occurred to her. She leaned over the deck railings of Coral Hut and called out to Saffron, who was hanging a pretty stained-glass lantern above the door of Headquarters.

"I don't suppose you've come across any spare camouflage netting, have you?"

Saffron thought about this for a moment. "Nope," she called back. "But the spare blanket has a camouflage pattern, if that helps."

Coral nodded. It definitely would help. She collected the blanket and returned to the deck, where Nicks was preoccupied with studying the rest of the completed Cupid Company questionnaires they had on file. Coral silently chose a spot beneath the window closest to the red hut and shrouded herself in the camouflage blanket. Just the tip of her nose and the round silver lens of the camera poked out (but only someone with super-hawk eyes would have noticed). And then Coral waited.

"I think we should reconsider Zinaida for Harry," said Nicks after a while.

The green mottled blanket beneath the window grunted.

Nicks was thoughtful. "Yes, she's a really nice girl." And then she glanced up. "Coral?"

The blanket grunted once more.

"CORAL!"

A hole appeared in the blanket, filled with Coral's bright red face. "How can I be undercover and have a conversation with you at the same time?" she snapped.

Nicks stared at her friend. "Why is your face that colour?"

"Probably because it's a hot day and I'm sitting under a blanket."

"Why?"

"I'm undercover. And it's all they had next door."

"Coral, I don't think being undercover means you actually have to be under cover."

"But I can't let Scary Guy see me. Or the camera." She jiggled the camera through the hole as proof.

Nicks nodded like she got it, even though she wasn't sure that she actually did. And then

Sienna suddenly appeared at the top of the deck steps.

"So what time do you expect Ramone today?" she asked directly.

Nicks shrugged. "I'm really not sure."

"Will Coral know?" said Sienna as she peered inside the hut.

"No, she won't," said the blanket in a muffled voice.

Sienna stared closely at the blanket. "Is that you, Coral?"

"Ummm."

"Why are you under a blanket?"

The blanket split open and Coral's frustrated (and even redder) face reappeared in the opening. "I'm *trying* to go undercover."

"Oh, right." But Sienna didn't seem to care enough to ask why. "So you don't know when Ramone will be along then?"

"No, I don't."

Still Sienna stared.

"Sorry," added Coral, who did still want to be

friends with the older girls.

Sienna turned on the heel of her silver satin pump and called out over her shoulder as she left, "Thanks, anyway!"

But she never quite made it back to her own beach hut, as she spied Ramone and Grace cycling along the promenade first.

"Ramone!" she squealed happily.

The other girls at Headquarters immediately all glanced up from what they were doing. Chanel reached for the compact mirror in her bag. Saffron ran a hand through her styled hair. Tallulah quickly applied another stroke of lipgloss. And then they all sat and waited with their shoulders back and their chins dipped daintily forward, like it was the most natural thing in the world.

The pair of Beach Patrol bicycles stopped near the huts. Ramone dismounted skilfully while Grace tumbled gracelessly from her bike. Ramone removed his helmet, dropped his chin and shook out his head of shiny dark curls before strutting boldly down the path. Grace fiddled with the clasp of her helmet, gave up and stumbled after Ramone with her helmet still on her head.

"We have arrived!" announced Ramone in a deep, booming voice.

"Hi, girls," chirruped Grace with a small wave of her hand.

Everyone stood up, except for Coral, who was determined to remain undercover (she would show the Beach Patrol just how serious she was!).

"I said we'd return," growled Ramone, his legs stretched wide apart like he was steadying himself for an earthquake.

The girls at Headquarters gave a collective sigh.

Grace slipped her notebook from her back pocket and prepared to write. "So have there been any new developments?"

Nicks glanced at the lump of blanket, but kept silent and shrugged instead.

"Well, I think we may have a mouse,"

announced Saffron with a coy smile and a helpless expression on her pretty face.

Ramone glanced back at the sand dunes covered in wild grass nestled behind the beach huts. He paused for a moment, his handsome silhouette pressing a shadowy outline into the glowing orb of the sun, and then turned back to the girls with fiery eyes. "It's probably a wood mouse. You'd better let me take a look," he said bravely.

The blanket lump grunted its annoyance. This was not lost on Grace, who stopped writing.

"Where's Coral?" she wondered.

The top of the blanket suddenly erupted and spat Coral's fire-hot face out into the open air. "I am *trying* to conduct undercover surveillance!" she howled as she shot upright. The blanket spilled across the floor like lava.

"You'll need to be a little less rowdy for undercover surveillance," suggested Grace calmly. "And just what were you looking for exactly?"

"Certainly not a wood mouse!" barked Coral, who was suddenly feeling rather fed up.

Grace turned to Ramone, who had already disappeared in the direction of Headquarters.

"We're trying to keep an eye on Scary Guy," admitted Nicks loyally.

"The owner of the red hut?" confirmed Grace as she scribbled once more. Nicks nodded.

"And what's the latest?"

The question dissolved Coral's fury. Finally somebody was talking business. She wasted no time in telling Grace all about the book called *Famous Copycat Murders* before finishing by asking her whether she thought that Scary Guy could be a copycat murderer.

"We mustn't jump to conclusions," replied Grace nervously. "Your neighbour remains innocent until proven guilty."

"I know all that!" Coral stamped a foot and punched the air excitedly. "And that's why we're here!"

But Grace just shook her helmet-head

slowly. "No, we're here to get to the truth – not to prove somebody guilty."

"Er, sure. Whatever." Coral retrieved the camouflage blanket from the floor. "Now, shall we all climb under together?"

"I don't think so," said Grace. "I will take a walk and speak to a few of the other beach hut residents."

"Oh, right." Coral nodded. "You're going to ask them if they've also seen Scary Guy acting suspiciously. Good idea."

Again Grace shook her head. "I'm not going to mention Scar— uh, your neighbour at all. Remember, we have no proof he's done anything wrong. I'm just going to ask a few general questions."

Coral was disappointed, but then remembered that a little of something was better than a lot of nothing. "OK, great. So where shall we start?"

Now it was Nicks's turn to shake her head. "Hey, we can't just go swanning off whenever we feel like it. Remember we have Cupid Company business to see to. Harry is stopping by tomorrow, and we can't let him down again."

Coral stared at her friend incredulously. *Like was she being serious?!*

"Oh, don't worry – you girls do what you have to do. This is Beach Patrol business. It's my job, remember?" And then Grace laughed at herself. "Well, it's not actually my *job*, seeing as I'm a volunteer, but you know what I mean."

Still Coral stared, her eyes growing wider and wider.

"Oh, Coral, don't overreact," snapped Nicks. "And Grace is right – it's Beach Patrol business anyway. And Harry is Cupid Company business."

Now Coral's mouth grew wider too.

"Is she all right?" whispered Grace.

"I've got it!" yelled Coral triumphantly.

Grace took a step back. Coral certainly had something, but there was no saying if a dose of crazy was contagious or not.

"Grace and Harry are perfect for each other!" Coral shrieked. "They're about the same age. And they both really care for the community and for Sunday Harbour!"

Nicks thought about this for a moment. She tried to find holes in Coral's suggestion. Matchmaking was usually far more complicated and scientific. But after a while even she had to admit that it was a rather good suggestion. Both Grace and Harry were passionate about their community volunteer work. They were both gentle and kind. They even both had a sort of cool geekiness about them. In fact, it was a mystery how they hadn't found their way to each other already – without the Cupid Company's help.

"Good thinking, Coral," she finally said out loud.

"Hello, I'm still here," said Grace with her hand raised in the air. "And who is Harry, and what exactly is it that you are plotting for us?"

"Harry volunteers with the Community

Alliance and the Beach Huts Association," explained Coral. "He's looking for a girlfriend. Maybe you've seen him around? He's very nice. And very honest."

Grace looked blank. So Coral raised her own hand in the air. "He's about *this* tall. With brown, sticking-up hair. And nice eyes."

"Hold on, I have his Cupid Company questionnaire right here," said Nicks. She reached for the sheet with Harry's scribble across the top. "Here we go. Firstly, Harry is passionate about protecting marine life."

Grace gave an interested nod. "I washed seals after the oil spill."

"Harry hates litter," continued Nicks.

"I regularly help to clear rubbish from the shoreline," admitted Grace.

"Harry is a vegetarian."

Grace smiled. "I won't even wear leather shoes."

"So you see – you're perfect for each other!" cheered Coral.

Grace frowned and scratched the helmet on her head while she stared out wistfully. "Mmm, but Ramone…"

Coral followed her gaze over to the man in question. He was sprawled out on a blanket and enjoying a neck massage courtesy of Tallulah. "Oh, Grace, not you too," she groaned.

Grace shrugged irritably, like it really wasn't her fault. "But he is kind of cute."

"So are wood mice. But some creatures are better set free," groaned Coral. "Ramone is just one more reason why you should definitely go on a date with Harry."

Grace thought about this for a moment. The fact that her up-until-now-secret crush was clearly enjoying being surrounded by a group of pretty girls seemed to make her mind up for her. "OK then, I'll do it!" she decided.

"Great, we'll set it up for you," replied Nicks in a firm, businesslike tone as she slipped Grace a questionnaire. "Now, if you would just fill this out please—"

"Don't worry about that now," interrupted Coral. "We've got Scary Guy business to see to first. We have to go and speak to the beach hut residents. And I'll bring the camera along too."

cold·hearted

Interrogating the rest of the beach hut residents proved to be a huge disappointment for Coral. They found out nothing useful; nobody had even noticed anything unusual in the vicinity. But then Grace had refused to mention Scary Guy to any of the residents, and she had only asked very general questions in her usual mild manner. Coral would have done things very differently. When Ramone and

Grace finally left they were no closer to solving the case of Scary Guy.

Coral sat on the deck of Coral Hut, rubbing Romeo's belly and sighing every so often. She couldn't help thinking about Scary Guy. Still, there was some good news: the Cupid Company was doing rather well – they'd got Grace to agree to go on a date with Harry. Now all they had to do was convince Harry to go on a date with Grace. And true to his word, it wasn't very long before Harry came trundling along the promenade. He climbed the steps to Coral Hut and smiled expectantly.

"Well, here I am!" he announced, his arms spread wide open like he was just waiting for love to fall into his lap.

Coral glanced around for Nicks, who was much better at the actual organisational side of Cupid Company business, but her best friend was nowhere to be seen. She was a serial sea-dipper and obviously still dipping herself in the warm salty sea.

"We have found you a great girl!" revealed Coral in the meantime. "Her name is Grace, and she is very excited to meet you too."

Harry grinned and tested out her name. "Grace. Mmm. When do I get to see her then?"

Coral's gaze swept the beach once more, looking for Nicks the organiser. "Um, I'm not quite sure. But soon. Very soon."

And then, from out of nowhere, Scary Guy appeared. His tall head suddenly and unexpectedly floated right past the deck of Coral Hut. He was walking slowly and talking angrily into a mobile phone.

"I'm free today," said Harry, who had barely even noticed the passer-by.

Coral froze. Even her lips froze, but still she managed to tell Harry to "Shhh!" She tipped forward; it was the first time she had actually heard Scary Guy speak.

"You've gone too far," he snarled into the phone. His voice was a sinister growl.

Silence.

"They don't call me Doctor Death for nothing!" he fumed.

Silence.

"Yeah? You think so!" he raged at the voice in his ear. "Well, we'll see about that. You will be very sorry!"

Scary Guy a.k.a. Doctor Death was already at the door of the red hut, but he was shouting loud enough for both Coral and Harry to hear him quite clearly. And then he disappeared inside his hut.

Coral and Harry stood, stunned and silent.

Then the door of the hut flew open once more and Scary Guy stomped down the deck steps and across the beach, growling and muttering to himself along the way until finally he had disappeared again.

Harry chuckled uncomfortably. "Doctor Death – I'm glad he's not my GP." And then he chuckled some more.

"It's not funny." Coral's head turned slowly. "Harry, do you realise what that was?"

Harry shrugged. "One severely annoyed doc?"

"No, that was a DEATH THREAT!"

Harry tilted his head at an angle, just in case he hadn't heard correctly.

"Did he or did he not say," Coral paused to take a deep breath, "*They don't call me Doctor Death for nothing, you will be very sorry*?"

"Well, he didn't say it together like that, but yes, that's what he said, I suppose."

Coral realised that both she and Harry were now witnesses to the death threat. And if Harry was going to be any sort of witness he would need the full background story to Scary Guy. So she told him everything – from the roll of duct tape to the book on copycat murders – in the precise order it had taken place. Of course she placed special emphasis on the weapon in his hut. A knife (even a penknife) was not something to be simply dismissed.

"Oh, right," was all Harry said when she finally finished.

"We must debrief Grace!" declared Coral.

"Would that be *my* Grace?"

"And seeing as we're both witnesses we'll debrief Grace together."

"But what about my romantic first date?" groaned Harry. Coral knew a debrief was obviously not quite the date he'd had in mind, but she could not let him wriggle out of it now. Not everyone believed her stories – she needed back up. And she would need it sooner than she thought.

She looked across the beach to where Nicks was now emerging from the salty sea. She dripped her way dry across the sand to the beach hut and appeared at the top of the deck steps. She took one look at Coral and Harry: something was quite obviously up. *And she hadn't even been gone for very long!*

"We just overheard Scary Guy making a death threat to somebody over the phone!" hissed Coral urgently.

"Really?" replied Nicks, directing it straight at Harry.

He shrugged uncertainly. "Well, that is what it sounded like," he admitted.

Nicks stayed silent and glanced back to Coral and then back to Harry. She blinked a few times and then narrowed her eyes while she mulled the news over. Only then did she speak. "So you definitely heard this for yourself, Harry?"

"We were *BOTH* witness to the death threat!" cried Coral.

Still Nicks stared at Harry until he nodded his agreement.

"Wow," she finally said. "So what do we do now?"

"We'll report it to Beach Patrol. And they'll probably take the information, along with the case file, to the police," revealed Coral importantly.

Nicks chewed on her lip while she gave this some serious thought. "Well, if that's what you *both* heard then we should definitely find Ramone right away."

Coral made a 'pssht' sort of sound. "We'd better find Grace, I think."

"Yes, Grace..." murmured Harry. He was clearly crestfallen at the thought of his first date with this wonderful girl called Grace turning into a cold-hearted witness statement. And in spite of everything that was going on with Scary Guy, Coral couldn't overlook his disappointment. She stared and scratched her chin thoughtfully. Could she fix things so that she got her witness statement and Harry got his unforgettable first date too?

King of hearts

Grace promised to be over in less than two hours. They had time, but not a lot of it.

"Couldn't Harry and Grace just go on a date after you make your witness statements?" said Nicks.

"But that first moment between couples means so much," replied Coral wistfully. She'd seen most of the greatest romantic films ever made over and over, so she knew that first impressions counted for a lot. Meeting over a witness statement was not a story to share with your grandchildren. "We have to make it special," she said. "The reputation of the Cupid Company depends on it."

So she thought long and hard about love, for inspiration.

Love.

Sweetheart.

Hearts.

Valentines.

Her Valentine decorations! She'd used them to transform her bedroom into a shrine to love. It was now the most romantic place ever. And all they had to do was take the decorations down and transport them to Coral Hut. It was simple. It was genius. She was a genius! Coral grinned wider than the horizon curved over Sunday Harbour.

"Come on, follow me," was all she said to Nicks and Harry.

Usually Romeo simply followed without

being told, but today he stayed put, both front paws and the round tip of his black nose poking over the hut decking.

"Come along, Romeo," Coral called out. But still he didn't budge. She watched her pup for a moment. She knew what it was – he was feeling neglected. She had admittedly been so focused on Scary Guy and the girls next door that she really hadn't paid her beloved pet much attention recently. Come to think of it, she couldn't even remember the last time they'd played chase together. Suddenly she felt very guilty. But she would make it up to him, just as soon as they had the case of Scary Guy resolved. He would have to take the back seat for a little while longer; lives just might depend on it.

"How about a lovely biscuit?" she offered him as a temporary replacement for her full attention.

Romeo's ears pricked up. But still he didn't budge.

"How about a biscuit AND a bowl of milk?" The milk would be a very special treat.

Romeo leaped to his feet and gave one firm, sharp bark. A deal had been struck, and off they all trotted.

They arrived at Coral's house and made straight for the Valentine themed bedroom. There really was not a moment to waste. But even so, Harry could not help stopping and staring in wonder at the padded fabric hearts that spelled out BE MINE and LOVE BUG. He waded through the fake rose petals scattered across the carpet and gazed up at the dangling cupids and garland of red and silver foil hearts. He gawked at the heart stickers on the windows, gaped at the helium-filled balloons printed with L FOR LOVE and smiled at the giant banner that said I LOVE YOU. This really was a room dedicated to romance.

Coral busily retrieved the decorations' original box and placed it in the middle of the bedroom. "You get busy taking all this down," she instructed. "I have a bowl of milk to arrange."

Harry and Nicks didn't need to be told twice, and before long the bedroom was a bare and uninteresting shadow of its former heart-shaped self. But they now had a full box of decorations for Coral Hut. The clock was ticking; Grace would not be long. Harry carried the box and they raced all the way back to the promenade and the row of beach huts. Even Romeo seemed excited. Not only was he full of milk, but the sprint back to Coral Hut was as close to a game of chase as he'd had all week (not that anybody actually caught him, mind you).

Harry dumped the box on the hut's deck and they all waited a few moments for their breathing to slow.

"Right," puffed Coral as soon as she was able, "now you two get busy hanging the decorations and I'll quickly pop next door." And then she was gone again.

She found Saffron and the girls centred around a magazine, taking a *What's Your Wedding Style?* quiz.

"Hiya," she said.

"Is Ramone here?" shrieked Tallulah, throwing her magazine and the quiz into the air in panic. She quickly ran a hand through her unstyled hair and bit her unglossed bottom lip.

Coral sighed. "Nope. And no, I don't know when he'll be around either. But I have a favour to ask, please."

The girls seemed less interested once they knew that Ramone wasn't due for a visit. Coral pushed on regardless. "Do you think I could borrow some flowers and a few candles?"

The girls stared at her blankly and then Chanel's nose wrinkled up slyly. "Do you have a special play-date with a boy then?" she asked mischievously.

Now it was Coral's turn to stare balefully. *What was she – like five years old?* "No, I definitely do not," she said sternly, just to prove that she certainly would not even *want* a play-date with a boy. "But somebody else does," she added with a mysterious smile.

"It's not Ramone, is it?" asked Sienna nervously.

Coral quickly dropped the smile. "No, it's definitely not Ramone. So anyway, would you mind?"

"Oh, right, the candles and flowers," remembered Saffron with a nod. "Of course – just wait a moment."

It only took her a few moments to collect a pretty vase of fresh cream roses and a tray of tealight candles. Coral stared down at the offering; it would all do just perfectly.

"Thanks!" she called out over her shoulder as she quickly made her way back to Coral Hut, where Harry and Nicks had been hard at work hanging the heart-shaped decorations. The interior of the hut was already barely recognisable. It was bright and beautiful and even more romantic than before. Coral set the vase of fresh cream roses on the wooden straight-back chair beside the daybed and then placed the tealight candles strategically around the hut. Now there was only one thing still left to do. The bag of rose petals lay untouched at the bottom of the cardboard box. Nicks noticed it first and handed it over to Harry.

"Come on, you do it," she said with a smile. "For good luck!"

Harry grinned and carried the bag out to the deck, where he scattered the petals by the handful. Before long the outside of the hut looked wonderfully romantic too. He glanced up and grinned. "I think we're finally ready!"

sweethearts

It wasn't long before they heard the sound of a frantic yelp and a squawk as Grace's big, shiny bike veered off the promenade and back again, nearly flattening a seagull. She finally arrived at Coral Hut with a clatter and a groan, but she was all business, quickly tapping her back pocket seriously, just to check that she hadn't lost her Beach Patrol notebook along the way. Her small, satisfied smile said that the notebook was still in place as she made her way down the path to Coral Hut, using the opportunity to scan the ground for any potential Scary Guy clues they might have missed earlier.

It was a lovely summer's evening and the sleepy sun glowed a warm, soft orange colour. The sea breeze had already dropped and the beach was emptying, leaving only sandcastles and footprints on the cooling golden sand. Grace bounced down the path and up the hut steps. It was plain to see that she loved the beach at this time of the day, and she liked the girls at Coral Hut too. And then she came to a sudden stop. She stared at the rose petals scattered across Coral Hut's decking. This was very unusual. She quickly jotted it down in her notebook.

And then she continued on and into the beach hut. But instead of Coral and Nicks, a young man with dark brown, sticking-up hair and glasses sat on the daybed. And as if that weren't noticeable enough, the stranger was surrounded by decorations shaped like hearts. It was all very unexpected and unusual and she quickly made another note in her book. She then folded her arms and narrowed her gaze. Her training had prepared her for this moment.

"What have you done with Coral and Nicks?" she demanded firmly.

The stranger quickly stood up and hopped nervously from one foot to the other. Grace noticed it all; she wouldn't miss a thing.

"Uh, definitely, absolutely nothing," replied Harry nervously.

Grace gave the hut another once-over just to be sure. "So where are the girls then?"

"They'll be along soon," he stammered. "I'm Harry, by the way."

The name rang a bell in Grace's head. "Harry... hey," she murmured as she scribbled and then glanced up. She stared at the young man pensively while she rooted around her memory. "I don't suppose you're passionate about protecting marine life, are you?" she asked.

Harry nodded eagerly. "Oh, yes, very!"

Grace made another note and considered her next question. "And how do you feel about litter?"

"I hate the stuff!"

"Mmm." Grace bit the end of her pencil thoughtfully. "And do you prefer eating at steakhouses or burger bars?" This was her trick question.

Suddenly, Harry frowned. "Oh, neither! I'm a vegetarian," he confirmed with a nod.

Finally Grace forgot about her notebook. She looked up at Harry and grinned. "So this is a Cupid Company setup and you're my date?" she guessed. Harry shrugged bashfully and nodded once more. Grace laughed. "Well, at least it explains all the Valentine decorations!"

Harry laughed too. "The girls arranged it all and I helped."

"It's very pretty, thank you." And then she put her hand out. "It's nice to meet you, Harry."

Harry took her hand. "It's nice to meet you too, Grace."

And then they both stood silent and bashful. But it wasn't quiet for long. The sound of feet stomping up the deck steps quickly filled the air. Coral arrived, soon followed by Nicks. They both looked very pleased, especially Coral.

"So, that went well!" she cheered.

Both Grace and Harry's cheeks darkened to red. Not that Coral noticed – she was too focused on business. With the Cupid Company side of things taken care of, it was time to concentrate on Scary Guy business. They had a death threat to report.

"So we have more news on our neighbour," she began, looking to Harry for backup. But he was very busy staring at Grace with a silly grin on his face. "Harry!" she hissed.

"Uh, yes?" He tried to concentrate, but the

188

silly grin still lurked around the corners of his mouth.

"We should tell Grace about the death threat. Why don't you go first?" This seemed like a good idea; people didn't always take her stories seriously enough.

"A death threat?" echoed Grace, with wide eyes.

"Yes, we overheard the man who owns that beach hut..." Harry pointed to the glossy red hut. "He was talking into his mobile phone. He said his name was Doctor Death. And he also said that the person on the other end of the line would be sorry."

"But he didn't just *say* it, did he, Harry?" Coral pressed him.

"He didn't?"

"No, he yelled it – in furious anger. He was very angry. He was murderously angry. It was a very angry death threat."

Harry shrugged and glanced back at Grace. She paused her scribbling and stared up at the two witnesses in astonishment and wonder. This was the big time; it was the moment she had been waiting for. And this did not seem to be lost on Harry either. He raised his chin and straightened his spine.

"Yes, yes… he was very furious and very threatening," he agreed, watching for Grace's reaction. Her eyes pulled even wider. So Harry puffed his chest out and started pacing as he spoke.

"Coral and I were standing on the deck of this beach hut – talking about you, actually," he paused to direct the silly grin at Grace before continuing seriously once more. "And this tall, thin guy stormed past, shouting and waving a finger threateningly in the air."

Coral closed an eye and tipped her head thoughtfully. She must have forgotten about the waving finger.

"He kept calling himself Doctor Death," continued Harry dramatically, "and that's when I noticed that his pointing finger now resembled a pointing gun. You know, with his thumb up in the air like this." Harry demonstrated.

Coral scratched her chin. She must have missed the hand-gun thing too. Wasn't Harry the smart detective! Grace seemed to think so too, as she stared at him in obvious admiration.

"Anyway," said Harry, "I was at this point considering wrestling the guy to the ground. I mean, he was menacing. And there were children about. But then he suddenly disappeared inside the red beach hut. I think he must have noticed me watching. It was just as well I was there, I think." And then finally Harry stopped talking. They all remained silent with their thoughts.

Harry seems a little overexcited, reflected Nicks, *rather like Coral when she exaggerates a story.*

Isn't Harry like the best death-threat witness ever! thought Coral.

And Grace stood there awestruck.

So Harry sent her another silly grin.

heart of gold

Grace took their witness statements back to the Beach Patrol office and promised to be in touch very soon. After that, there was very little for the girls to do but wait patiently and keep a close eye on Scary Guy, just in case.

Not even a brand-new day could move Coral's thoughts on from the case. It was all she could think about. *When it's all over, will*

we get an award for bravery and good citizenship? It might even be a medal – with dangly ribbons. Perhaps they'll even name a street after me.

"You know you're not being very helpful!"

The voice collided with Coral's thoughts and smashed them to pieces. She focused her faraway eyes and found Nicks giving her a sideways glare.

"You've hardly helped at all," added Nicks grumpily.

"I've been picking up the petals," replied Coral, even though she was still standing toe-deep in fake red petals.

Nicks flung a padded heart into the cardboard box already half filled with Valentine decorations. "Well, you'll be at it all week if you don't speed up."

So Coral picked up two petals at a time instead of just one. She even did it double-time. Romeo decided the flurry of activity was the start of a game of chase and he nipped the

193

petals from Coral's grip and retreated in backward bounds.

"Oh, Romeo," groaned Coral, who found picking up the petals hard enough work without having to chase after them too. It wasn't her fault; all the worrying about Scary Guy had tired her out. "You know, I think I'd better sit down," she said.

Nicks hung her hands on her hips. "Why, what's wrong?"

"I think I've just been overdoing it."

Nicks harrumphed and took two strides over to her deck chair. "Well, if you've been overdoing it then so have I," she mumbled and sat down. She was feeling fed up with always being the responsible, just-get-the-job-done one.

Coral shook her head and smiled weakly, like she wouldn't hold it against her friend if she rested too. She settled her head against a cushion. But her rest would not last long.

"Hi, girls!"

She sat up straight and peered ahead. It was Saffron, and she was waving at them. Nicks slid off her deck chair and leaned over the deck railings.

"Nice day, huh?" she called out, and waved. Of course Scary Guy occupied some space in her head, but not nearly as much as her best friend's.

"It's the perfect day for a Best Beach Hut competition!" cheered Saffron in reply.

Nicks turned and stared at Coral, who stared right back.

"THE BEST BEACH HUT COMPETITION!" they both yelled out at once. With everything that had been going on, they had completely forgotten about it.

"Are you sure?" asked Coral hopefully.

Saffron nodded and grinned. "Of course! We've been waiting ages for it. And besides, it's our last day in Sunday Harbour. Birdie and the Captain will be back today."

This was a lot of information at once. No

more fabulous next-door neighbours. But they could look forward to the return of their old next-door neighbours. And what about the beach hut competition? This was their first summer at Coral Hut – how could they *not* enter?

"What time?" asked Coral.

"Birdie called to say sometime this morning," replied Saffron.

"No, what time does the competition begin?"

"The judges start making their way around the huts at two o'clock. So you've got to be ready!"

Nicks nodded distractedly. This was only a few hours away. They needed time to think, but Saffron didn't appear to be going anywhere.

"Look at what we found at the Seaside Store," she revealed.

She held a colourful WELCOME mat along with a miniature yellow beach-hut birdhouse in the air. She smiled. "They're our finishing touches. The girls and I just love makeovers!"

And with that she finally left for the beach hut next door.

"What are we going to do?" hissed Coral.

"We've got to do something!" moaned Nicks. "It would be letting Coral Hut and the Cupid Company down if we make no effort at all."

Coral agreed. They needed to think carefully. All they needed was some time. But it seemed like that was the one thing they would not get.

"WE'RE HOME!" sang a loud, rather familiar-sounding voice.

A quick glance was all that was needed to confirm Birdie's arrival. She still looked the same, only a little less suntanned. And she was still smiling as usual, although her smile did seem to be fading very fast. It only took a matter of moments for it to disappear completely, leaving in its place a look of confusion and disbelief. She stared at Headquarters, blinked a few times and then glanced over at Coral Hut, as if she was trying to get her bearings. Coral and Nicks waved uncomfortably. Birdie's hand fluttered as she tried to wave back, but the effort of it proved too much. All she could do was stand and stare at her beach hut.

And then the Captain appeared, marching left right, left right, down the beach in the direction of Birdie and their beloved beach hut. He appeared to be very glad to be back in Sunday Harbour. His mouth was turned up at the corners and he was breathing deeply and enjoying the beachy views so much that he almost collided with Birdie.

"Oh, do come along," he ordered kindly. "There's no time to waste."

But still Birdie didn't move. She just stared. So the Captain followed her stare. And then his jaw dropped to the sand.

"What in the name...?" he finally mumbled in a strained and breathy voice. Everyone knew that since the Captain's early retirement from the army because of a badly injured knee, the khaki beach hut called Headquarters had been his very favourite place in the world. It was all he had left of the army. It had been like his very own mini barracks. Only now it looked more like a sparkly girly hangout. He stared with desperate eyes. He seemed to be taking it hard.

Just then Saffron appeared at the door. She noticed her aunt and uncle and waved happily. "You're here!" she cried out. "And just in time – we wanted to have everything perfect for your return."

"You did?" gulped Birdie.

Tallulah appeared behind Saffron. "Yes, welcome back!"

"Don't you just love the beach hut!" cheered Chanel as she burst out on to the deck. They had been planning this moment and seemed very pleased to be finally showing off their hard work.

Birdie and the Captain gazed mournfully at the pretty pots filled with colourful flowers, the decorative window dressings, the dangly wind chimes and gleaming cut-glass suncatchers.

199

They could just about glimpse the interior of Headquarters too. Cream and gold stitched satin, scarves, feathers and silk flowers... It was not quite the hut they had left behind.

"We wanted to say thank you for letting us use your beach hut," explained Sienna.

"And we're hoping to win the Best Beach Hut competition for you too," added Saffron, "because we know how much you love your beach hut. Only, it was a little dull." She rolled her eyes at the sky above and giggled.

"Yes, quite," murmured the Captain sadly.

"But it's not dull any more, is it?" said Birdie with pleading eyes directed at her miserable husband.

The Captain remained silent for a few moments. It looked like he might cry (if he weren't such a big, strong ex-army sort of guy). But finally he coughed and pulled himself upright. He shook his head and set his jaw like he'd survived tougher situations than this one.

"No, it certainly isn't dull," he finally replied quietly.

"So you love it!" cheered Saffron.

Birdie smiled nervously and glanced over at the Captain. For a while nothing happened. And then he forced his mouth to curl up. He cleared his throat and straightened his spine. "Yes," he said finally, "we do love the hut."

Everyone clapped, including Birdie. Her eyes were shiny as she blew the Captain a kiss.

heart·warming

It was a lovely day – not too hot and not too breezy, and the Captain abruptly left for a brisk run down the beach. Nicks and Coral watched him leave with a smile; it was good to have their old neighbours back. And the Captain must have missed his beachy jogs because he was planning on running all the way down to the cove and all the way back again. He was going to be gone for quite some time.

Meanwhile, the older girls all buzzed around each other excitedly. Birdie made sure to "Ooh" and "Ahh" politely at the khaki beach hut's new decorative touches. She listened patiently to the stories about their big-city-girl seaside escapades. And then finally she made her way over to Coral Hut.

"The Captain and I certainly have missed you girls," she said with a smile.

"We missed you too," replied Nicks, almost shyly. Romeo gave two eager barks to show that he'd been doing some of his own missing too. Birdie was very giving when it came to doggy treats.

Birdie gazed around Coral Hut, which was still half dressed in foil hearts, dangling cupids and balloons that spelled L FOR LOVE. "Oh, my, you are making a brilliant effort for the Best Beach Hut competition!" she cried out in admiration. "It suits the Cupid Company perfectly, and the judges certainly won't find another hut like this one."

Coral and Nicks turned to each other with giant eyes. And then they both giggled crazily. Sometimes the most obvious things took the longest to notice, even when they were right under your nose all along! Love was a bit like that too.

"We hope the judges feel the same way you do," said Coral with a grin, like it had been their plan all along.

"I hear there's a special celebrity judge this year," Birdie revealed. "Everybody is talking about it."

"Who is it?" gasped Coral, who was a big fan of celebrities.

"I have no idea. But I do know that this person has recently moved to Sunday Harbour."

Coral thought about this for a moment. She felt that it was unlikely that she'd have missed a proper big-time celebrity living in Sunday Harbour. But she didn't want to doubt Birdie either, so she simply kept quiet and nodded civilly. The so-called celebrity was probably the presenter of *Gardener's World* or something…

If Birdie had noticed Coral's skewed mouth she didn't let on. She scooped up a handful of rose petals and blew them over the girls playfully. "It is good to be back!" she sighed happily. "Now, I'd better go and help the girls next door put the final few finishing touches to Headquarters."

They watched her leave and then stared at the box they'd half filled with decorations and now had to hang once again. Not that they minded one bit – they couldn't wait for the judges to see their beautiful hut in all its glory. So they got very busy, saying little while they worked. They hung things and decorated and polished and swept the hut while they thought about the celebrity judge. They finished just in time too, ready for her. Or him. *If there really was a celebrity judge at all…*

The girls watched as the judges made their way along the promenade, pausing at each hut as they went. Coral narrowed her gaze and stared hard, searching for signs of a celebrity. She hoped for bodyguards and bling. She prayed for fans and photographers. So far she saw none of these things.

Finally the touring group reached Headquarters. They were now close enough for Coral and Nicks to scrutinise the judges and yet they still couldn't spot the celebrity. The mayor of Sunday Harbour was there and wearing a long floral dress. She was bookended by two bald men. One was tall and round, the other was shorter and round. And then there was a man in a pale yellow suit and matching hat. He looked very much like the *Gardener's World* sort.

Nicks jabbed an elbow in Coral's side. "Hey, there's Harry," she said. Not that they were surprised to see him. He did, after all, work for the Beach Huts Association.

Harry sent them a secret wave. He then glanced left and right, tucked his neck into his shoulders and slipped away from the group without being noticed. He crept up to Coral Hut and grinned broadly.

"Hi, girls!" he hissed hoarsely. He checked on the mayor, who was still admiring the pot plants at Headquarters, and then looked past the girls into Coral Hut. "I can only be a moment. I don't suppose Grace is here, is she?"

Coral and Nicks both shook their heads. "She should be along soon though," added Nicks.

"So where is the celebrity judge?" Coral whispered, just in case there really was an A-lister nearby (she didn't want to seem desperate).

"Oh, right. The celebrity judge is coming…" said Harry distractedly, with a trace of disappointment in his voice. "Soon… very soon. You'll have to wait until the prize-giving," he added, scanning the beach just in case Grace had arrived in the last five seconds. He really did seem smitten, and very little else except

Grace appeared to interest him much.

"Just WHO is this celebrity judge?" demanded a now desperate Coral.

But Harry's attention had already returned to the mayor, who had finished admiring the pot plants at Headquarters and was looking around like she was lost. The other judges didn't seem to know where to go either.

"Oh dear, I've gotta dash," said Harry. And then he was gone. The girls watched as he wheedled his way back in beside the judges, smiling and calmly sweeping a hand in the direction of Coral Hut. The judges nodded and smiled. There was a lot of smiling. And then finally they arrived at the pale pink, minty-green and lemon-yellow painted beach hut.

Coral and Nicks stood with their feet together and their hands tucked neatly at their sides. They were, after all, in the company of the mayor of Sunday Harbour (even if she wasn't a proper celebrity). They were just as keen to impress the other judges too. They were even more eager to win the Best Beach Hut competition. Coral stretched her smile as wide as it would go, while Nicks lifted the corners of her mouth until her smile found her eyes.

The mayor nodded politely at the girls and then stared around at the decorations dedicated to love. Her face softened and her eyes turned misty. Coral and Nicks understood. After all, what girl did not love 'love'? The two bald men and the man in the yellow suit and hat soon followed, which suddenly made the deck of Coral Hut very crowded. Coral and Nicks pressed their backs against the railings to let everyone pass. The taller man hit his bald head on a dangling cupid and the man in the yellow suit seemed more focused on his trousers than the hut. He cocked and kicked his right leg in an attempt to dislodge some of the fake rose petals that seemed to have climbed inside the cuffs of his trousers. The shorter bald man was having troubles of his own. The balloons that spelled L FOR LOVE were at perfect head height and, thanks to a breeze that had come up, he was being boxed around the ears.

But the mayor did not seem to notice any of this. She seemed most impressed with their beach hut dedicated to love. "Very nice, very nice," she murmured with a gentle smile and a nod of her head. And that was when she noticed the Cupid Company sign on the wall.

"The Cupid Company?" she wondered out loud.

And Coral was ready. She took one bold step forward and wasted no time delivering a detailed description of the Cupid Company's motives and services. She even had a few business cards ready in her back pocket and she handed one out to each of the judges. They all stared at the small squares of card with rough scissor edges in dismay.

"Oh yes, we can *even help you*," responded Coral. "You're never too old for love. That's, uh, if you're – you know – like not already married."

She had just spied the glint of a wedding ring on the yellow-suited man's finger.

Nicks rolled her eyes and coughed loudly. She would have kicked her best friend's shins if her foot was long enough.

"Well, thank you very much for the tour," replied the mayor. She led the trail of judges back down the beach hut steps in the direction of Harry, who was still waiting with a jolly face.

"The next hut is not entered into the competition…" the girls heard him say as the group of judges strolled past the red beach hut.

"What are you like!" squawked Nicks, at the first chance she got.

"I know," replied Coral with a satisfied smile. "I just don't miss an opportunity. It's like I was born to do this. Sometimes I feel like Venus the goddess of love. I'm quite sure I was destined to help the world find romance…"

But Nicks wasn't listening. She had already disappeared inside Coral Hut, making a 'tut-tut' sort of sound as she went.

hearts in the right place

There was already a crowd building on the beach. Almost all of Sunday Harbour's beach huts entered into the Best Beach Hut competition had been judged and very soon the judges – including the mystery celebrity judge – would return to the flagged area on the beach. This was where they would present the prize to the winner and the runners-up.

Everyone was very excited and chattering

loudly in anticipation of the big event. Still, it was impossible to miss the sounds coming from the khaki beach hut next door. The four girls were primped and lipglossed and twittering, ready for the judges and the first prize, which they felt confident was theirs. Coral was less focused on the Best Beach Hut competition and more interested in the potential celebrity who would be arriving soon. The mystery surrounding the guest judge had captured her imagination. She was no longer convinced that the celeb had anything to do with *Gardener's World*. In fact, the more she thought about it, all signs pointed to an A-lister (why else did nobody seem to know anything about this famous person!).

Out of the girls next door, Tallulah seemed to be the most excited, growing louder as the minutes ticked by.

"Sunday Harbour will surely never forget us. There's nothing like going out with a bang!" she sang happily, as if the winning prize was theirs already.

Sienna seemed a little less chirpy. "I will miss the place," she grumbled, straining her gaze down the length of the promenade as if she was searching for something. Or someone. Coral suspected that Sienna would miss Ramone more than she would miss Sunday Harbour, but she forgave her instantly. After all, she would miss the fabulous big-city girls so much, and she really wanted them to come back again soon (so maybe it really wasn't so bad that Sienna was all gung-ho over Ramone).

But instead of Ramone it was Birdie and the Captain who next made an appearance. They returned to Headquarters after visiting their beach hut neighbours, where they'd been catching up on all the beach hut news from the past few weeks. Birdie was still smiling at a story she'd heard, but the Captain seemed less smiley. His mouth was an upside-down shape.

"I think I'll go for a run," he said gruffly.

"What – again? And must you go now, darling?" replied Birdie with surprised eyes.

After all, it was almost time for the Best Beach Hut prize-giving.

"Yes, I must," was all he said before setting off at a brisk pace.

Birdie looked like she might call him back, but then she seemed to change her mind. He was already halfway down the beach and besides, she was distracted by a sudden *crash-bang* sound. Everyone, including Birdie, instantly turned in the direction of the clatter. It sounded like somebody had fallen off a bicycle.

"Hi, Grace!" Nicks called out.

They'd been waiting for her return. And this time she'd brought Ramone with her. The girls next door beamed excitedly. And then they remembered themselves and quickly toned down their grins to sultry, smouldering pouts. They stood up straight, tucked their tummies in, and showed their best sides. Coral sighed. *They were fabulous!* Nicks seemed less bothered by their fanfare and more interested in Grace.

"Are you OK?" she asked.

Grace nodded and then shrugged sheepishly. "You get used to the bumps and scrapes," she replied, like she'd long since accepted that she would forever remain *graceless*.

Ramone nodded at Coral and Nicks and then immediately swaggered in the direction of Headquarters, only pausing to strike a pose – biceps flexed – when the sun hit him at the right angle.

Coral shook her head and turned back to Grace. "So do you have any news on Scary Guy yet?"

"Sorry, not yet. But I've made a case report and left it with my superior. Now it's up to the big guns." She shrugged once more, like it really was out of her hands.

Coral and Nicks were disappointed. They'd been waiting already. Now they had to wait some more.

"I don't suppose Harry is around, is he?" Grace asked innocently.

Nicks managed a small smile. "Well, he was

here, but he left again with the judges." Grace slumped. "He should be back very soon though," she added.

Grace grew a little taller again and looked pleased. They were all distracted by the sound of Sienna suddenly screeching with laughter, and snapped their heads in the direction of the khaki hut. Ramone was now lying on a blanket on the patch of sand in front of Headquarters. He was stretched out and propped up on one elbow while the four cooing big-city girls took it in turns to feed him chocolate. Coral shuddered and turned away. She had expected better from them (well, not from Ramone, but from the fabulous girls certainly).

"There's Harry!" whispered Grace excitedly.

And sure enough, there he was, leading a small bustling group that consisted of the mayor, a few judges and some other people that were still too far away and too bunched up for Coral to see very clearly. She watched them closely though. One head in the centre of the group was much taller than the rest of the heads. It was even taller than the yellow hat of the yellow-suited judge.

The crowd seemed to grow more and more excited as the group drew closer to the flagged area and the prize-giving platform. They had been waiting for this moment. Beach hut owners grinned like they'd already won, and the rest of the chattering crowd jostled to get a better look. It wasn't often that a celebrity came to Sunday Harbour.

The judges' group shuffled closer and closer. Coral still watched the tall head. It definitely belonged to a man. And there was something strangely familiar about him. But then that was the thing about celebrities: they were famous. They were well known. So of course there would be something familiar about them.

The head grew more and more life-size as it moved down the promenade. And that was when Coral noticed that it wasn't just one head, but two. Well, sort of. That was how it looked, anyway, because the man had a giant Adam's apple. *IT WAS S-C-A-R-Y G-U-Y!*

Coral screeched out loud.

"What's wrong?" gasped Nicks.

Coral had stopped breathing, which made speech impossible. So she pointed instead.

Nicks tracked the direction of her friend's trembling hand. Big yellow hat... *S-C-A-R-Y G-U-Y!*

"HIT THE FLOOR!" yelled Coral just moments before she belly-flopped on to the hut decking.

"What are you doing?" Nicks hissed.

"SCARY GUY!"

"Yes, I know. But why are you on the floor?" Nicks just did not get the beached-fish impression her friend was doing.

"He's Doctor Death! We must keep safe!"

Nicks stared calmly across the jostling crowd to Scary Guy. The judges' group was now close enough for her to see everything quite clearly.

The mayor was staring up at their gangly beach hut neighbour with sparkly-eyed admiration. The tall, bald judge was grinning like they were very old friends and patting Scary Guy's back. The man in the yellow suit and hat was also trying to walk as close to him as possible. People in the crowd stretched out their hands holding autograph books and pens as he passed. Somebody even held a huge poster in the air. It was simple in design and featured a large black and white photograph of Scary Guy with writing at the top and bottom. Above the photo it said, J.D. HATCHETT IS DOCTOR DEATH. The printing at the bottom of the picture said the rest: AWARD-WINNING CRIME THRILLER WRITER. Yes, it seemed as though Scary Guy was definitely Sunday Harbour's big celebrity.

Moments from the past few weeks played over in Nicks's head like a speeded-up movie. She watched Scary Guy (also known as Award-Winning Crime Thriller Writer) drop his bag containing rope and duct tape. Then she was back inside his red beach hut with the chalkboard that said things like SUFFOCATE, STRANGLE, THROW BODY OVERBOARD and POISON. She remembered his desk and the cup filled with pencils and piles of papers covered in scrawl. And there was that book he'd dropped: *Famous Copycat Murders*. So all this time... he'd been doing nothing more... than researching... and writing... He was, after all, Doctor Death.

Nicks's mouth stretched wide. Then she chuckled. And before long she was hooting with everything she had inside her.

Coral was still hugging the decking when she heard her friend lose her mind. She stared up at Nicks, who was now fever-red and doubled over with hysterical laughter.

"Oh, stand up!" gasped Nicks to her friend when she was finally able. "Coral, get up! Scary Guy isn't a mass murderer after all. He's a crime writer. Look!"

Coral got up slowly and stared straight

ahead at the J.D. Hatchett posters. She glimpsed the excited fans standing with hardback copies of his novels open on a page ready for his autograph. She also took notice of the devoted fans wearing their Doctor Death T-shirts.

She thought about it all and then thought about it some more (although it wasn't easy to be contemplative with Nicks's cackling in the background). She had just about worked it all out when Scary Guy, a.k.a. J.D. Hatchett a.k.a. Doctor Death, took a deep breath and held a finger up in the air, as if he was about to make a point. But then he seemed to be distracted by the bandage round his pointed finger. He shrugged sheepishly.

"For some reason I still use a penknife to sharpen my pencils," he explained with some embarrassment (like not only had he not yet discovered computers, but he hadn't even found his way to using a proper pencil sharpener either). He shrugged again. "I guess

I'm just old-fashioned."

But the mayor seemed to think he was marvellous, and cheered him on. Scary Guy, a.k.a. J.D. Hatchett a.k.a. Doctor Death, seemed uncomfortable with all the fuss and attention though, as if the only reason he'd moved to Sunday Harbour was to find some peace and quiet. He seemed very eager to get this all over and done with.

"And the winner of the Best Beach Hut competition is…" he continued.

But Coral wasn't even listening. She was still tangled up in the thoughts in her head. She tap-tapped her chin thoughtfully. *Mmm… so it appears that I've been right all along.*

"What a clever cover-up," she murmured slowly. "Yes, pretend you're a crime thriller writer to hide your murderous trail. That's criminally clever."

She turned to let Nicks in on her genius realisation. The crowd was suddenly cheering loudly. Nicks was bobbing up and down and clapping excitedly. Saffron, Sienna, Tallulah and Chanel were all equally excited and blowing kisses to the crowd.

Coral watched her best friend's grinning, slowly moving lips. "We got joint first place!"

Joint first place? Coral considered the news for a moment and then turned slowly to face the crowd again. She could see Grace smiling sweetly at Harry, who now had his arm draped casually across her shoulders. And not too far away Ramone leaned in close and whispered into the ear of the giggling Russian girl Zinaida. The Captain returned breathless from his run and Birdie greeted him with a hug. And Romeo sat silent and hopeful at the feet of the mayor, who was now delicately nibbling on a snack. Everyone seemed happy and carefree. It was time to celebrate Sunday Harbour's beautiful beach huts. Coral shrugged. Then she grinned. Now celebrating – that was one of her very favourite things in the world!